A KILLER
IN THEIR MIDST

A COZY MYSTERY IN THE WILDERNESS

Liz Turner

Contents

Chapter 1 Old News...5

Chapter 2 Unusual Guests 11

Chapter 3 Fishing 101 20

Chapter 4 The Witness 31

Chapter 5 Bad Landing..39

Chapter 6 Watery Escape 49

Chapter 7 Catching Rats 61

Chapter 8 Ghost Town...69

Chapter 9 Wolves 80

Chapter 10 More Rats...90

Chapter 11 A Special Visitor 100

Chapter 1
Old News

They shroud the New York Supreme Court in the color of mourning after losing one of the state's finest lawyers.

Alfred Waters, the well-known district attorney, was found dead last night on a downtown New York street . Waters was heading the infamous case against one of New York's suspected gang leaders, Leo Romano. It is believed that Waters was about to make a breakthrough in the upcoming trial against the Romano family gang. Waters' unexpected death has placed the prosecution team in a frenzy to pin the guilt on the Romanos. However, there has been no legitimate evidence to support this theory.

Leo Romano spoke to the press this morning, appearing shocked to hear of Waters' passing. The stone-faced family patriarch, accused of many heinous crimes, gave way to tears before a stunned crowd of media representatives. After a series of shouted accusations, Romano claimed he and his wife were out for dinner at a local restaurant, thus providing a score of reliable alibis.

Romano offered his sincerest condolences to the Waters family and prayed they would bring justice to the "scum who took out a worthy opponent like Alfred Waters."

While the FBI offered no formal statement, witnesses who found the body commented that Waters was stabbed several times in what appeared to be a "mugging gone wrong." A bystander observed that Waters' wallet was lying on the sidewalk untouched, indicating that the killer was after more.

The officers investigating the murder will neither confirm nor deny whether there were any witnesses. However, it is rumored that a child witnessed the entire incident.

The newly widowed Mrs. Waters refused to talk to the press and has not been seen at her home since the announcement of her husband's death. It is believed Alfred Waters had a young son who was reported absent at school this morning. No representative from the family has made themselves available for a formal interview.

The highly anticipated case against Leo Romano, which has been eagerly followed by the citizens of New York, will reconvene at a later date, after prosecution has had time to recover from the enormous blow of losing Alfred Waters. It is said that Waters' assistant prosecutor will step into the coveted position of District Attorney temporarily or until –

"What's got you so absorbed?" a voice interrupted Charlotte's morning news intake.

"I wish we lived in New York." Charlotte sighed and folded up the newspaper, slapping it onto the table in front of her.

"You wish you were anywhere else but in the raw beauty of Northern Canada," her husband mumbled over the brim of his coffee mug.

"That's not true! I love my life here." Charlotte stepped closer to the enormous window covering the wall and framing the spectacular outdoor vista that breathed with life instead of pollution.

Rather than skyscrapers disappearing into the clouds, tall, dark pine trees rolled out as far as the eye could see, wind rustling through their needles as they curved around the shores of Lake Athabasca. Eagle calls filled the air as they soared over the lake, whose waters reflected the puffs of drifting white clouds above. Those same clouds carried the threat of an unexpected summer storm with the power to transform the peaceful setting into a raging torrential downpour at any moment.

This was the life Charlotte looked out at, day after day.

Oliver looked up from the fishing book he'd been reading, his eyes finding his wife gazing out the window. "What are you thinking about?"

It took Charlotte a few seconds to pull herself away from the view. She serenely smiled back at him. "I was just thinking about how much I love running a lodge my husband built with his own hands. I love fishing on those chilly waters with you, hauling in a twenty-pound trout, and cooking it up on a fire on the shore." She kissed him on the cheek. "I even love tracking my children through the woods, praying they haven't been eaten by a bear."

"Then what's bugging you?"

"Nothing," Charlotte mumbled, staring at her shoes.

Oliver's expression grew stern. "Charlie, I know you. I can't tear you away from the guests when they arrive with stories from the city. When Nick brings the newspapers, you're as excited as Amelia on Christmas morning, even though the papers are two weeks outdated by the time we get them."

Charlotte folded her arms. She couldn't deny that when their pilot friend, Nick, arrived with news from the states, she got giddy with excitement. But comparing her to their youngest daughter, who crowed like a rooster at the crack of dawn on Christmas mornings, was a little extreme. "Don't you ever wonder what life must be like somewhere else?" she asked, knowing her husband always went on the defense about his beloved lake.

He settled his dark eyes on her and waited for her to explain further.

"Like the court case, for example..." she continued.

Oliver raised an eyebrow. "What court case?"

Charlotte gestured to the newspaper laying on the table between them. "There's a huge case going down between a gang in New York and the prosecution..."

Oliver shook his head and sighed.

"What? I haven't even started explaining."

"I just don't understand how reading about some awful gang that probably sells drugs and murders people, attracts you to the world beyond, when you have so much beauty in the clean life that surrounds you here."

Charlotte bit her lip. She knew her husband was right. She would never want to live in the city but she just thrived reading about it. "I can't explain it. It's just that life there seems so fast-paced and exciting. It seems more real. There's so much happening every day, whereas here..." Her gaze drifted to the window. "Here we get excited when a storm rolls in. It's just too tranquil."

Her husband walked over to put an arm around Charlotte's petite frame. "Our life is plenty exciting. Three beautiful children who constantly keep us on our toes, a crazy staff who always seems to have relationship problems, and visitors from all over the world. Not to mention the fishing."

Charlotte grinned. "I do love fishing."

Their moment was suddenly disturbed, however. Madison Le Blanc, Charlotte's assistant, burst into the room. "Olly!" she yelled before noticing their embrace and pausing awkwardly.

"It's all right." Charlotte smiled at her, separating from her husband. "What's up?"

"Wolves!" Madison squealed. "Somehow, they made their way into one of the guest cabins. Bill said one has already stolen his shoe, and he needs back-up."

Oliver frowned. "It's not like Bill to need backup, so this must be serious." He exited the room and headed towards their gun safe.

"Is it the whole pack again?" Charlotte asked, her eyes fixed on Madison.

She nodded. "I saw quite a few of those shaggy demons, and they looked more annoyed than usual."

Charlotte sighed. "Better get my gun too then…"

Oliver returned to the dining room and thrust Charlotte her rifle. "You wanted more excitement?" he teased. "How does chasing out a band of invasive wolves with a personal vendetta against us measure up on your list of exciting things to do today?"

Charlotte rolled her eyes. "When it's the third time this month, it gets a bit old." With a mock yawn, she slung her rifle over her shoulder. "I think we should try taming them instead. Amelia has always wanted a pet wolf."

"Great idea," Oliver said. "Who gets to tame wolves in the city?"

Chapter 2
Unusual Guests

Charlotte walked the perimeter of their lodge camp, dropping to her haunches at regular intervals to examine the rocky soil for unwanted paw prints. The lodge was expecting a new group of guests that afternoon, and Charlotte doubted the refined city folk would appreciate encountering vicious, hungry wolves in their cabin.

"It's not every day you get to declare war on a local gang of wolves," Bill teased, stepping out of the tree line. "Is that exciting enough for you?"

Charlotte grinned at him. "Hey, old man."

Some months before, the worn-out, weathered man had found his way from Uranium City—an old abandoned mining town—right to their front door. Bill claimed to have been working on the mine before it was shut down and had run out of money waiting for the mines to restart. By the time everyone else had packed up and left, he could no longer afford to find his way home, if there even was still a home waiting for him. Charlotte could never get the whole truth out of him and had simply pieced together what she could from his vague details.

Bill kept very much to himself, though he lent an immensely helpful hand around the lodge. Charlotte suspected he had a dark past that he was unwilling to reveal, and so she left him to his secrets. Her kids, Thomas in particular, had grown very close to Bill, and Bill found he had unknowingly stepped into the shoes of beloved grandfather, whether he wanted to or not.

"I guess Olly told you about my conversation with him," Charlotte said, embarrassed.

"Not in so many words," Bill replied, noticing the pink in Charlotte's cheeks. "You know Oliver. He doesn't exactly talk much."

Charlotte nodded, realizing how similar Bill and her husband were. "I suppose you think I'm silly for wanting a little more excitement in my life?" She averted her gaze, not wanting Bill to sense how much his opinion meant to her.

"Not at all. In fact," he gave a deep sigh, "I was like you once."

"What do you mean?"

"I longed for a life of adventure and excitement. But once I had left to find adventure, I realized that I'd left my most important adventure behind..."

Charlotte groaned. "I know what you're getting at. You think I should be content with what I have while I have it."

Bill shrugged. "More like you should try to enjoy the adventure you're already on."

"I'll keep that in mind," she said, and then diverted the subject. "Are you excited for the new guests arriving later?"

Bill nodded, a small smile finding its way onto his face, though most of it was concealed by his bushy beard, which had regrown almost overnight. "I'm selfish," he admitted, sniffing the air deeply and surveying the surrounding landscape.

Bill and Charlotte had walked up the little hill overlooking the lodge. Nestled below, they could see the ring of wooden cabins in the clearing, which housed the guests. Perched on stilts at the edge of the lake was the larger log cabin that contained the reception and dining areas, kitchen, and recreation room. To the left rested the staff cabins, and to the right was the creaky old boathouse containing a treasure trove of fishing rods, tackle, and other gear.

Benjamin, the head fishing guide, kept the boathouse in pristine condition, with everything labeled and packed in its place. The lodge owned a small fleet of eighteen-foot flat-flooring boats with pedestal seats and rod holders for the avid fishers who flew halfway around the world to fish the Athabascan waters.

Charlotte and Bill's eyes were drawn away from the man-made cabins towards the sparkling waters of the enormous lake that shone like a jewel in the midday sunlight.

"What do you mean you're selfish?" Charlotte asked.

Bill gave her a sideway glance. "Unlike you, I don't like sharing this with the world. I like to keep it safe and sacred—a place for the ones I love."

"Well, when you live in a place that's only accessible by boat or plane and only has a terrible radio line for communication, I'd say it's pretty safe and sacred compared to the rest of the world," Charlotte joked.

Bill shrugged. "The only reason they travel here is to experience a few days of the incredible beauty, warmth, and life that you get to live every day."

Charlotte nodded, absorbing the beauty around her. Yet, she couldn't help feeling it was a familiar beauty she could describe blindfolded, and that the world contained other beauties for her to discover.

Before her thoughts could take her any further, three child-sized figures darting out of the main lodge's window distracted her. Charlotte stared in shock as her children bolted from the building and hid under an overturned boat.

Bill spotted them too and barely disguised his guffaw as a cough. Moments later, a frantic Rebekah—who was supposed to be tutoring the children in mathematics—sprinted out of the front door, her head snapping left and right.

"I don't understand why they can't get through a single day without putting their tutor through hell," Charlotte complained.

"What time are the guests arriving?" Bill asked, attempting to turn her attention away from the children.

Charlotte jolted, instinctively checking her watch and seeing it was later than she realized. She scanned the skies as the unmistakable sound of an engine reached her ears. She raised a finger and pointed into the far distance. "There," she said. "I'd better get everyone ready for the greeting. Nick will march them up in the next fifteen minutes."

Bill grinned. "I'll go catch your children and return them to their warden."

Charlotte scanned the line of staff members waiting excitedly to greet the new guests who'd soon be making their lodge a home for the rest of the week.

Madison, an array of blonde curls cascading around her face, was at the forefront. She lived on the unrealistic, yet undying hope that her soulmate might walk through the lodge doors one day, swoop her up into his arms, and whisk her away into a life of happily ever-after content.

Close to Madison was her rival, Rebekah Martin. Rebekah served as both tutor for the children and head housekeeper, yet she seemed to win the favor of any male Madison set her eyes on.

Behind the two flirtatious young women stood the head chef, Victor Fournier, rolling his eyes at the incessant giggling erupting from the girls as the predominantly male group of guests approached. "Could the two of you shut up?" he hissed between his thin lips.

Madison rolled her eyes. "Are you jealous that we don't giggle this much over *you* anymore?"

Victor shook his head and sneered. Victor had rejected both women on many occasions, but he also didn't relish being ignored either.

"Smile everyone," Charlotte said, her head darting around to check if her husband was still in his position.

Oliver was gone, as usual. Charlotte was used to being the lone face of the lodge. Her shy husband preferred to work behind the scenes, where no one could see or talk to him. On rare occasions, he would step into public and befriend the odd tourist that he found he could be himself around. But when a group was arriving from the city, he disappeared for days, claiming he had nothing to say to them.

She turned her attention back to the approaching group. They looked smaller than they were supposed to be. Naturally, Nick, their pilot, was at the forefront of the group, though Charlotte noticed he wasn't wearing his default of overconfidence.

Charlotte watched as Nick's eyes scanned the familiar staff group until they found Madison, at which point his standard grin found its way back onto his face. He'd been openly in love with Madison for years.

"Welcome to the Northern Getaway Fishing Lodge and Retreat Center!" Charlotte said excitedly as the group reached them. "We're happy to introduce you to our staff here at the getaway, though we prefer to see ourselves as one extensive family —"

"Sorry," one man interrupted, stepping forward, "I'm in charge of my group, and we don't really have time for your little introductory speech."

"Doug!" a pale woman chastised. "Don't be rude. The woman was literally mid-sentence."

"Jeez, Doug, you don't have to be such a butt," another man said. He stepped forward and Charlotte thought Rebekah and Madison would faint when he winked in their direction. He was tall, dark haired, and had a compelling air about him. He extended his hand to Charlotte. "I'm Trevor, but you can call me Trev."

"Nice to meet you," Charlotte wormed her fingers out of his tight grip and addressed the entire group. "I'm Charlotte Bouchard. My husband, Oliver, and I," she gave Trevor a firm look until he stepped aside, "run this place together." She then turned her gaze to the first man, Doug. "I understand that you would like to hurry things along. Can our chef serve lunch?"

"Thank you," Doug answered curtly, his face slightly red from being called out by Trevor. "I apologize for my abruptness, but we have some urgent business we need to attend to."

"Oh," Charlotte stammered. "I thought the group was here for fishing or other activities?"

"There will be none of that. We need a large room where we can set up office without being disturbed. We've got some…" he hesitated slightly, "filing that we need to attend to while we're here."

"Of course." Charlotte nodded, ever the perfect host, though she could sense the staff's disappointment. "We can set you up in the recreation room. Now, before lunch, I'm sure you'd like to freshen up. Madison and Rebekah will show you to your cabins."

Charlotte maintained her poised smile as the group hastily departed. She noticed Trevor was soon escorting Madison and Rebekah to the cabins rather than the other way around. Victor stormed off into the kitchen, and she could hear him slamming pans onto the stove and cursing at his assistant.

"They're a dry bunch," Nick commented, sidling up to her. He knew perfectly that Charlotte didn't approve of him and his reckless flying skills. But he was one of the few men brave enough to pilot the precarious storm-raging skies of Saskatchewan.

"What do you mean?" Charlotte asked, studying the odd group. It comprised two men who seemed at odds with each other, a woman who looked as though she hadn't slept in a week, and a small boy who was determined not to make eye-contact with the adults around them.

"They hardly said a word on the flight over. And instead of having their noses glued to the windows, admiring the nature beneath them, they sat huddled together, casting furtive glances at each other. I was even too scared to flirt with the woman in case they tossed me out of my plane."

Charlotte snorted. Nick being too afraid to flirt with someone had always seemed like an impossible occurrence. "Am I mistaken, or was the booking not supposed to be for six?" Charlotte checked her roster.

"Oh, I thought so too. When I asked them, they got really weird about it and said the other two would join them on the weekend. So, I'll fly out again and return to deliver the precious cargo."

"They strike me as out-of-place here. We've had no guests who spent the entire time indoors, unless we forced them to by the weather."

"What gets me," Nick added conspiratorially, "is that they don't even look comfortable in their holiday clothes. I'm no conspiracy theorist, but it's like this is all some bizarre cover for something."

Charlotte laughed again. "I guess city folk are more comfortable in suits and ties. What could they possibly be covering up?"

"I don't know what your take on aliens is," Nick responded, deadpan, "but these guys look like some undercover extraterrestrial agents."

Charlotte bit her lip, but it was no use. She dissolved into uncontrollable laughter that sent tears streaming down her cheeks.

Annoyed, Nick shrugged her off. "I'm going to check out your bar. Tell Madi I'm around for a late-night drink if she's interested."

"She's never interested, Nick," Charlotte said, wiping away her tears.

"She will be one day," Nick said as he disappeared into the recreation room.

Chapter 3
Fishing 101

Charlotte tried to study the odd group as discreetly as possible. The men shoveled down their breakfast with enormous mouthfuls, pausing only to whisper to each other behind their hands.

The woman, named Sandy, pushed her scrambled eggs around on an otherwise empty plate. She clearly had no appetite and looked as though she hadn't slept at all. She cradled a third cup of coffee between her hands and appeared oblivious to the young boy next to her.

"Mommy," he tugged at her sleeve and looked at her with his big brown eyes, "can I go play outside?"

"No. It's not safe outside. Besides, you need to think about what you want to say."

"What about fishing?" he asked. "I hear there are plenty of boats we can go out on and learn to fish. *Please*! Daddy always promised he'd teach me how to fish..."

"Well, Daddy's not here," she snapped before softening her expression and extending a trembling hand to caress his shoulder with apology.

The boy folded his arms and stared down at his plate, his ears red and his eyes glistening with unwelcome tears.

Charlotte noticed she wasn't the only one observing this scene play out.

Her eldest son slowly crossed the room, his sneakers squeaking on the polished wooden floorboards. "Excuse me, ma'am," Thomas began politely, "I'm Thomas. My mom and dad work here."

Sandy fixed him with a blank stare, but the boy's face looked up in interest. "I'm Nicolas," he piped, extending a sticky hand.

"Shh," his mother scolded and then turned to Charlotte's son. "Thomas, we're fine, thank you."

"Oh, sorry," the boy mumbled. "I forgot my name is actually Sam."

His mother rolled her eyes. "Just eat your breakfast," she muttered.

"I can take Nicolas, or Sam, fishing, if you'd like," Thomas offered. "My friend, Bill, can keep us safe, and I can teach Nicolas how to fish."

The boy's brown eyes lit up, and he turned to his mother, his fingers stroking her arm as he pleaded with her to let him go.

"Okay," she finally conceded, her shoulders slumping in defeat. "But only for a little while."

Charlotte quickly made her way over to Sandy and the two boys. "Sandy, I hope Thomas isn't intruding on your privacy, but I think that it would be good for the boys to get outdoors and enjoy the beautiful scenery. Bill is knowledgeable about these surroundings and can keep the boys safe."

"I said it's fine. I could do with some peace, anyway."

Nicolas didn't visibly flinch, but Charlotte could see the hurt in his eyes. She leveled a cool gaze on the frail, disinterested woman before escorting the two boys out of the dining area. "Let's see what Victor can wrap up for you two to take on your fishing trip," Charlotte whispered in their ears.

"This place is so cool!" Nicolas exclaimed on the way to the kitchen. "Have you lived here your whole life?"

"Yup." Thomas gave a proud grin. "I was born and raised here."

"Thomas just turned fourteen, Nicolas. How old are you?" Charlotte asked.

"I'm nine," Nicolas responded, his head snapping in all directions, absorbing his surroundings.

Charlotte pushed open the door to the kitchen. The warmth from the ovens and stove heated their cheeks instantly, and tantalizing aromas wafted over towards them.

Victor appeared through a puff of steam. "What you are smelling," he gestured to the surrounding air, "is dessert for tonight." He gave a smug smile.

"It smells wonderful!" Nicolas said, his nose practically lifting him off the ground.

Victor's eyes flickered to the young boy. "How was the breakfast received?"

"The guests don't seem to care all that much about food," Charlotte replied, perplexed. "I know," she added in response to Victor's horrified expression. "I don't understand it myself. Let's hope dessert changes their mind tonight, though. If anyone can convert them into food lovers, it's you, chef."

Nicolas smiled meekly and tugged Victor's sleeve. "I loved it."

The usually stern and aloof Victor dropped to one knee, leveling himself with Nicolas. "Thank you, young man. Now, what brings you into my kitchen this morning?"

Nicolas's smile grew. "I would like some snacks to go fishing with."

"Did you know that the Athabascan trout love marshmallows?" Victor asked, his face dead serious.

"Really? Is trout a fish?"

"Wait…" Victory scratched his three-day-old stubble. "I think it's the fishermen who need the marshmallows. And yes, trout are fish. You have a lot to learn, little man."

Thomas laughed, realizing the joke. Moments later, Nicolas caught on and giggled too.

"Victor, would you mind packing them a lunch box? Bill is going to teach our city boy how to fish," Charlotte said, unused to seeing the chef behave in such a courteous, calm fashion.

With a nod, Victor whisked away to pack a fully loaded picnic basket.

"What's life like in the city?" Thomas asked, turning to Nicolas.

Nicolas shrugged, his face growing dark. "It's not like here," he concluded with a shiver that raked his entire tiny frame.

"What do you mean?" Charlotte asked, taking interest in the conversation.

"I feel safer here," Nicolas explained.

Thomas flicked his eyes to his mother, as if sensing Nicolas's answer wasn't exactly normal for a nine-year-old. He then turned his attention back to the boy and grinned. "I'm not sure what you have to be afraid of in the city, but we have wolves and bears here."

Nicolas's eyes widened and he attached himself to Charlotte's leg.

"He's teasing," Charlotte assured, giving her son a stern look. "We take every precaution to make sure that you're safe here."

Seconds later, Victor returned with a basket stuffed with ham sandwiches, fruit, muffins, and lemonade. "Just in case you don't catch enough fish to cook and eat." He winked.

Charlotte stared open-mouthed at the chef. Victor could be the most condescending man at the lodge, and yet around kids, he transformed into one himself.

"Thank you, chef," Charlotte announced, the two boys echoing her.

After escorting the boys to the shore where Bill had immediately begun explaining the intricate workings of a fishing rod, Charlotte made her way back to her office. She had a lot more time on her hands than usual when guests were around, which she was unused to. Hence, she figured she could use the extra time to get on top of her accounts and receipts that needed to be filed.

As she turned the handle to her office, however, she heard the radio inside. She pulled the door opened and found a strange man. "Excuse me?" she said, shocked.

The man jolted and spun around. It was Trevor, his face a mask of surprise. "Oh, sorry..."

"What are you doing?" Charlotte hurried to her radio set and turned it off. "This room is off limits for guests."

"I didn't realize that." Trevor nervously swiped a hand through his hair.

Charlotte narrowed her eyes at him. "Did the 'private' sign on the door not give it away?" Her eyes scanned her desk, checking if anything was out of place. No one had ever stolen from her before, so she wasn't entirely sure what to even look for.

Trevor took a step closer to her, his smirk rigidly fixed in place.

In return, Charlotte backed away, her hand reaching into her top desk drawer for bear spray.

"I have a confession…" Trevor said, smirking.

Charlotte blinked. She had never been alone in a room with a strange man advancing on her before.

"I came here to find you," he continued.

"Why? Is there something wrong with your cabin?"

"Everything in my cabin is fine." His eyes probed into her, focusing on her every move. "So, have you always lived here?"

"I moved out here after I married my *husband*. And together, we've built this lodge."

Trevor scoffed. "I have yet to see this husband of yours. How do I know he's real and you're not just playing hard to get?"

"Hard to get *what*?" Her fingers felt for the bear spray and curled around the cylinder.

Trevor's eyes flashed to her hand. "Is that bear spray?" he asked in shock while backing away.

Charlotte shrugged, embarrassed that he'd noticed her reaching for it.

"Look, I'm not some kind of weirdo," he said defensively. "I think you're a beautiful woman, and just wanted to talk to you."

Charlotte's heart pumped rapidly and her hands were sweaty. "I made it perfectly clear when we met yesterday that I have a husband."

Trevor shrugged, his dark hair falling over his eyes as he gave a boyish grin. "There's no harm in trying to get to know someone you admire. I mean, you're pretty impressive, Charlotte Bouchard."

She clenched her jaw, more uncomfortable by the second. "I don't think this is appropriate."

Trevor laughed. "I guess things up here are a lot more severe. Back in the city, men and women can be friends without strings attached." His eyes settled on hers.

Charlotte had chased away a pack of wolves on her own before. She'd come between her three kids and a bear raiding their picnic basket. She had even dived into the deep, icy waters of the Athabascan Lake to pull Amelia out after she'd fallen overboard. She felt ill-equipped to deal with the unwanted flirtations of a man she barely knew. "I think it would be best if you leave," she choked out, her light brown eyes blazing.

Trevor raised his hands in innocence, his lips twitching into an amused smirk. "You can't blame a guy for trying." He casually strolled towards her, pausing to level his lips with her ear. "If you were my wife, I wouldn't allow you out of my sight." And with that, he headed out the door.

***

"What's wrong with you?" Oliver asked as he entered the office fifteen minutes later.

Charlotte sat on the edge of her desk, staring at their radio, her cheeks flushed with guilt.

"Hey," he asked gently, "what's with the face?"

Charlotte's eyes welled with tears. She wanted to tell her husband about Trevor's advances, but she had a feeling how Oliver would react; anyone who encroached on his family was cast out without a second thought.

She took a deep breath. "I caught Trevor in here trying to use our radio. He's one of the guests…"

Oliver furrowed his brow. "That's odd. What do you think he was trying to do?"

Charlotte shrugged and stared at her boots.

"Did something else happen?" Oliver came closer and took a seat next to her.

"He may have flirted with me a bit," she confessed. "Though I can't really be sure what his motives were."

Oliver wrapped an arm around her, drawing her to his chest and clinching her. "I'm sorry, love. I've kept my distance from this group. I shouldn't be surprised that some big city hot-shot thought he could come in here and whisk you off your feet."

"He made me feel so stupid." She wiped an angry tear from her face. "He pretended his advances were perfectly normal, and I was the weird one for not reciprocating."

"We're in a safe place here. We're one extensive family, and we know and trust each other. But it's not like that everywhere. People want what they want, and if they can't get it, they take it."

Charlotte shook her head. "I guess I wouldn't last a single day in the city."

Her husband squeezed her tighter. "Do you want me to punch him in the face?"

Charlotte laughed.

"What?" Oliver teased. "I think that's how they go about things in the city."

Charlotte sighed. "No, just ignore it. I'm wondering if he was really interested in me at all."

"What do you mean?"

"He was fiddling with the radio. What if he was trying to send a message somewhere?"

"What would be so wrong with that?"

"Nothing." Charlotte shook her head. "It's just that I think this group values their privacy. I feel like they don't want anyone to know what they're doing here."

Her husband gave her a bemused look. "Have you been listening to Nick's alien theories?"

"He told you about that too?" She rolled her eyes. "Look, dear husband of mine, you'd actually have to spend over five seconds in the same room with them to see for yourself."

"Sorry," he mumbled. "I just can't stand city folk. Especially ones that are undercover alien agents."

She nudged him in the ribs with her elbow, a laugh escaping her lips.

***

Douglas eyed Charlotte with a snarl. "What was so important that you had to drag me away from my… rest time."

Charlotte scowled, but bit her tongue. Douglas had been alone in the recreation room when she'd found him. He'd hurriedly snapped the lid shut on the box he was working in as soon as she had creaked the door open. "Sorry to disturb you," she began. "I gather the nature of your business here is very private."

Douglas frowned immediately on the defense. "What are you talking about? Clearly, we're on holiday. I just have some light filing to do."

"I see." Charlotte nodded primly, though she didn't buy his story. "I thought it might interest you that one of your colleagues… I mean friends," she corrected herself when she saw his expression, "was in my office, trying to use our radio."

A vein throbbed in Doug's forehead.

"I just thought you might want to know that." Charlotte shrugged.

"Do you know if he reached anybody?"

Charlotte shook her head. "I don't know. I think he was still looking for the right frequency. I turned it off when I found him. Maybe he was simply trying to contact the rest of your group arriving on the weekend…"

Douglas scratched his chin. "Where is the boy?"

"Nicolas?"

"Yes. I mean, no… Sam." He cleared his throat awkwardly. "I haven't seen *Sam* all morning."

"He's out fishing with my son… They're perfectly safe."

Douglas shook his head. "You have no idea," he said, and then hurried out of the room.

Charlotte stared after him, tiring of being left in the dark in her own lodge. She might not know how to ward off unwanted attention from flirtatious men, but she knew people. No matter which part of the world they came from, people were still people and therefore all the same, carrying the same innate flaws as the rest of humanity.

Under normal circumstances, Charlotte would never poke her nose into affairs that didn't concern her. But at the moment, she could tell something was wrong.

Holding her breath, she dropped her gaze to the box on the table. Before she realized what was happening, her fingers found the lid and pulled it off. She took out the top file, exhaled slowly, and flipped open the front cover.

Her eyes scanned page, reading and rereading the lines in disbelief.

Chapter 4
The Witness

"What are you doing?"

Charlotte's gasped and dropped the file to the table. "I might ask you the same question," she managed after finding her voice.

Douglas stared at her, while Trevor advanced and ripped the box and file away from her.

"How dare you search through our things!" Sandy snapped.

"What kind of establishment are you running here?" Douglas demanded, his fist and jawline clenched in fury.

"The kind that has the right to know what's going on!" Charlotte retorted, holding her ground.

"How much did she see?" Douglas asked Trevor.

"Not much," Trevor replied. "Trust me, a girl like her wouldn't know what she was reading even if she went through the entire box."

Nicolas was hiding his face in his mother's skirt, peeping out now and then. Meanwhile, Sandy continued glaring at Charlotte.

Douglas, however, relaxed somewhat. "Look, Charlotte," he directed his full attention to her, "can you just trust that we have something of the utmost importance that we're dealing with? Something that you wouldn't understand. We need the quiet and safety of this place, simply because nobody knows where it is or how to get here."

Charlotte nodded slowly.

"I would advise your discretion," Douglas cautioned, the threat clear in his voice.

"Relax," Trevor said. "She has no clue what's going on."

Charlotte raised her chin. "Do you mean the Romano court case in New York?" she asked, against her better judgement. They met her question with deadly silence.

Trevor stared at her open-mouthed, shocked.

"I might not be from the city," she continued defiantly, her ego bruised, "but I can read the newspapers. I've been following the case for months now." Charlotte directed her gaze to Douglas. "I'm guessing you're the new district attorney taking over for Waters. That makes you some kind of assistant in the prosecution team..." Her eyes lingered on Trevor.

Douglas and Trevor paled.

Sobs from the corner of the room drew Charlotte's attention. She focused on the exhausted Sandy and the crying Nicolas, who still had his head nestled in her skirt. "I'm sorry for your loss, Mrs. Waters," Charlotte said gravely.

The recently widowed Sandy Waters averted her gaze, her fingers finding her son's head as she rubbed his hair.

"What I don't understand though," Charlotte resumed, "is what you're doing here?"

Douglas came to her side and lowered his voice. "We needed somewhere safe, isolated, and off the grid."

"Why? You're all big shot lawyers. Can't you just disappear in New York? Why drag yourselves all the way out here?"

"The case is of a rather delicate nature right now," Douglas answered, accidentally giving himself away. His eyes flicked to Nicolas before dropping to the floor.

Charlotte gasped again, her eyes finding Nicolas and realizing what the little boy had been through. "No!"

"Sandy, take Nicolas to clean up," Douglas ordered.

Sandy gave him a hurt expression but obeyed, leaving the room with Nicolas trailing behind her.

"The boy!" Charlotte breathed in utter shock. "That's Alfred's boy!"

"Yes," Douglas confirmed sadly. "Can you understand why he needs to be out of the city? Too many reminders."

Realizing Douglas was trying to prey on her ignorance once more, she shook him off. "Don't start that again. I'm not stupid. I know it was insinuated that a young child witnessed the murder of Alfred Waters."

Douglas shot Trevor a nervous look.

"Nicolas saw his father get killed, didn't he?" Charlotte said, her sentence being cut off in a well of emotion. "He's the witness!"

"I know it's a lot to comprehend," Douglas whispered, "but that little boy's life depends on how well we can protect him."

"Why bring him here? We don't have any federal agency that can swoop out and rescue him if things go wrong!"

"What do you mean?"

"The nearest corporal is over fifty-five miles away in Fond du-Lac! There's no immediate help here."

"That won't be necessary," Douglas insisted. "No one knows Nicolas is here. We got him out of the country immediately, under a different identity. As long as our stay here remains private, he's perfectly safe until he can disappear into witness protection for good."

"Safe from who?"

Trevor raised his eyebrows and Douglas scratched his head, realizing the error in his words. It was slowly dawning on both men they had presumptuously underestimated their host.

"I have a family that also needs to be protected," Charlotte pointed out. "I have three children of my own and I will *not* have them getting caught up with murderous gang leaders trying to silence a witness!"

"Calm down." Douglas tried to lay a reassuring hand on Charlotte's arm, but she shrugged away from him. "You've been reading too many novels. It's not like that."

Charlotte folded her arms. "It's amazing how gullible you think we are just because we live out here. I might not be used to people lying to my face, but that doesn't mean I can't spot a liar when I see one."

"All right," Douglas raised his voice. "You're right. There's considerable danger. If the Romanos get hold of Nicolas, he's dead. That's why no one can know we're out here. But what are the chances that a city gang is going to track us all the way into Northern Canada, of all places?"

"Well," Charlotte turned to glare at Trevor, "why were you trying to use the radio?"

Trevor sighed. "I was trying to get a message to the rest of our group traveling up this weekend, okay?"

"Once the rest of your team arrives, you catch that flight out of here, understand?" Charlotte stated firmly.

"Charlotte," Douglas addressed her gently, "a little boy's life is at stake. What would you do if he was your son? What would you do if someone had stabbed your husband over a breakthrough in the last court case he ever worked? I can see you've got an enormous heart, otherwise, you wouldn't be this involved in your guests' lives. Help us, *please*."

"I can see why you make an excellent lawyer," Charlotte responded half-heartedly, though his words had softened her heart. "I'm afraid the decision will lie with Oliver. He has a right to know, but I'll speak for you."

"Thank you." Douglas smiled, taking her hand in his and shaking it gently.

Charlotte pulled her hand away, still unwilling to trust any of the unwanted guests. But she thought of Nicolas tugging at his grieving mother's sleeve. She couldn't imagine enduring what Sandy and Nicolas had been through—losing a husband and father, and having to leave everything behind to keep safe.

Her desperate thirst for city life had been quenched with foul-tasting reality. "I'll send in some coffee and sandwiches so you can continue working the case," she offered.

"Thank you," Douglas and Trevor said in unison, relief radiating off them.

"Uh, Charlotte?" Trevor tugged her sleeve gently. "A word, please, if you don't mind…"

"Sure." She followed him to a corner of the room.

"I just wanted to apologize for my behavior earlier."

"It was rather rude," she said, unwilling to let him off the hook that easily.

"I know." He ran his fingers through his hair. "But now you understand the pressure Doug and I are under. Alfred was our boss. Our friend… Our brother. He taught us everything we know as lawyers. We have to put the people responsible for this behind bars. I guess it all just kind of got to me and I was looking for a brief distraction to help calm my nerves."

"Try fishing," Charlotte advised dryly. "It's a better way to relax than flirting with a married woman."

Trevor snorted and Charlotte gave way to a light laugh too, glad the tension between them was over. She had to admit, she'd misjudged the group, unaware of the trauma they were enduring. She almost felt bad for forcing her way into their confidence, because she now understood it was a dark hole she would have preferred staying out of.

Charlotte's thoughts were disturbed by an excited Madison sneaking into her office with a hopeless simper on her pretty face.

"Oh no…" Charlotte put down her mug of tea, already sensing the ensuing conversation.

"I'm in love, Charlie," Madison squeaked, fanning her face with her hands.

"Madi, please don't tell me it's not—"

"It's Trevor!" Madison gushed, pulling a chair until her knees practically touched Charlotte's.

Charlotte sank her head into her hands. "Madison, I know that I say this about every man you show interest in, but you seriously can't go for Trevor."

"Look," Madison's face grew serious, "I know that you got off to a poor start with Trevor, but he's not a bad guy. In fact, he's just the man I've always wanted."

"Oh really?" Charlotte looked up. "In what sense?"

"Well," Madison continued dreamily, "he's a pediatrician and does a lot of charity work at orphanages. I can just tell that he's genuine."

Charlotte shook her head. "Madi, he's not a doctor. I'm not saying he's a bad guy, but I'm telling you right now, he's not telling you the truth."

Madison groaned. "You *always* say that!"

"And I'm always right. The last guy you thought was the one committed attempted murder while he was here..."

Madison rolled her eyes and muttered under her voice.

"Please, just promise me you'll stay away from Trevor," Charlotte said. "He's not good for you. He's just looking for a girl to relax with while he's here. That's it."

"No strings attached, right?" Madison pouted. "Now that I think back, he used words like that..."

Charlotte nodded, grateful to see the truth dawning on her friend. "You're worth more than a weekend fling. Come on, Madi. I know you want someone to love, but don't settle for something less than you deserve."

Madison's Barbie-blue eyes filled with tears and she sobbed noisily for a couple of minutes before wiping her smudged mascara. "I know you're right. I just can't help hoping every guy who walks in here might be for me..."

Charlotte reached over and hugged her friend. "He might be right under your nose," she whispered.

"Nick?" Madison retorted in horror. "I'll never be *that* desperate."

Charlotte shrugged. "He's not that bad once you get to know him."

"He told me that Trevor was an undercover agent representing another planet!"

Charlotte snorted. Once again, Nick had removed himself from Madison's eligible bachelor list. "Well, you'll find the right guy, eventually. Now, I believe we have new guests to prepare for."

"Do you know if any of them are—"

"Don't you dare ask if there are any men."

Madison laughed. "Sorry, I can't help it."

Chapter 5
Bad Landing

"So, your pilot is due to arrive today," Douglas informed.

Charlotte paused from folding serviettes. "I'm aware of that. He's bringing another three guests from your group."

"He's bringing a lot more than that," Douglas said, his eyes darting around the room to ensure they were alone.

Charlotte raised an eyebrow. "Why do I not like the sound of that? What are you not telling me? And don't pull your lawyer act on me."

Douglas rolled his eyes. "Fine. Hamish and two others from our team are bringing some evidence through."

"That sounds harmless enough. What's the problem?"

"Well, it was the same evidence that got Alfred Waters killed."

Charlotte tossed her unfolded serviettes aside, her eyes widening. "*What*?"

"Alfred called me the day he died and left a message. He claimed he'd discovered a break in the case. He had found a way in..."

"Do you have any idea what it was?"

"All he said was that he uncovered conversations that would implicate the Romano gang in a lot of their accused wrongdoing."

"Where are those conversations now?"

"I suspect Alfred was meeting with a man on the inside to get the needed evidence."

"And that's when he was stabbed to death…" Charlotte concluded.

"I just don't understand why Alfred went alone that night. And why one earth would he have taken Nicolas with him? Nothing about that day makes sense." Douglas frowned. "Alfred never made mistakes. He was the best lawyer I knew. There's no way he would make a dangerous meet with his kid in the backseat."

"So your team that's flying up today, did they locate the taped conversations?"

"I assume so. Hamish was only supposed to meet us here if he had located the needed evidence. And since they sent word that they would be travelling, he must have tracked down what Alfred was after."

Charlotte tried to process this information. Something seemed off, but she couldn't put her finger on it. "How do you know they aren't bringing the Romano gang to Nicolas?"

Douglas remained silent, as though this level of betrayal wasn't something he had considered. "I trust my team," he stated stubbornly.

"What if they have infiltrated your team?"

Douglas scoffed. "With all due respect, I think I know my team better than you do. I've worked with these guys for years, and our joint aim is to take the Romanos down."

Charlotte sighed. "Fine," she conceded, folding her arms. "Why are you talking to me about this, then? Surely this is all information for your team only."

Douglas scowled, slightly embarrassed. "I don't know why, but I trust you. And I'm talking to you about this because I need your help."

"With what?"

"It's for just in case," he added quickly, "but we need some extra manpower to escort that evidence from the landing."

"Oh. How much of it could there be?"

Trevor scratched his chin and avoided her gaze. "It's likely just a small box, but they already killed one man for it. I want no more blood being shed."

"But you said the Romanos wouldn't come out this way—"

"It's just a precaution. I know you have rifles stashed somewhere in this place. It's one reason we chose a lodge as remote as yours."

"In the middle of nature, remote means bears and wolves. You assumed we would know how to defend ourselves with this kind of stuff?" The words fell out of Charlotte's mouth, though her mind remained numb. "How dare you put this on us!"

She couldn't quite explain it, but she felt as though the big city had toppled out of the newspaper pages and into her peaceful lodge, wedging its way in and suffocating them all.

Douglas held up his hands. "It's just precautionary. I need you with us, not against us."

Charlotte scowled for a few seconds before leaving the room to unlock the gun safe. She returned with three, and Douglas eagerly reached for one. "Not a chance," she dismissed his outreached hand. "I might have agreed to help you, but trusting your team enough to put weapons in your hands is another ballgame entirely."

Douglas glared while she led the way out to the landing strip.

There was no room for a lengthy landing strip at the lodge, but Nick's plane had floaters. He would swoop down at stomach-turning speeds, drift down to land on the lake, and then idle his way up to the landing jetty with a huge grin on his face.

Charlotte, accompanied by her husband and Bill, followed Trevor and Douglas through the winding path running along the shore to the landing area. Through a gap in the treetops, Charlotte had seen Nick's plane descend for a landing. By the grumbling roar of his engine, they could tell he was nearby.

"I still don't understand why the heck we're meeting our guests with loaded guns," Oliver hissed, glancing around furtively.

"I'll explain everything later," Charlotte whispered back. "But you will not like it."

"Something doesn't feel right," Bill said, his eyes darting behind him and forward again.

The trees and bush line were dense during summer, allowing a limited view of what lay ahead of them.

"Wait," Bill said again, his cautious tone bringing them all to an abrupt halt. He held Charlotte back by the arm.

The entire group froze while Bill listened to the air. A high-pitched whistle pierced the silence, followed by an ear-splitting explosion.

Charlotte dropped to the ground, her hands protecting her head as a cascade of ashes and splintered wood rained down on them. Her lungs burned from the smoke. She tried to get back to her feet, but deaf from the explosion, she lost her to balance and fell to her knees again.

Someone lifted her up. Turning, she spotted her husband, his face a mask of panic as he pulled her towards him. Frantically, he felt every inch of her, making sure she was still whole. She could see his lips moving, but couldn't hear him.

Her eyes flashed from person to person, doing a mental head-count of their group. Douglas was just as bewildered as she was. Bill was already up and alert, scanning the trees for the source of the attack, accustomed to the sound of blasts from his years in the mine.

"Are you hurt?" her husband's words finally penetrated her ringing ear drums.

She shook her head. "What happened?" she screamed at Douglas.

"I don't know," he breathed, his strong exterior in pieces. "This has to be the Romanos!"

"Nick!" Charlotte screamed in panic, wrenching herself free from her husband's grip as she bolted up the rest of the path, her rifle firmly in her hands. She rounded the bend and screamed.

The landing was non-existent. Shards of wood and twisted metal lay scattered around her, while the rest of the jetty smoked as smaller fires burned out.

"What the heck happened here?" Oliver shouted as he caught up to Charlotte. "There was nothing that could have caused this accidentally."

"Can anyone see Nick?" Charlotte cried, trying to see through the smoke toward the lake.

"I'm here," came a distant call. "We're alive!"

"Nick!" Charlotte screamed in relief. "Are you hurt?"

"Apart from the ringing in our ears, we're fine," came the answer.

As the air slowly cleared, Charlotte could see that the plane had drifted out into the lake again. Nick hung out of the door, waving to them.

Charlotte raised her hand to wave back and felt something tug on the rifle tucked under her arm. She spun around in a flash and stared down at Douglas, who had his hand on her weapon. "What do you think you are doing?" she shouted, wresting her weapon out of his reach.

Douglas raised his hands in surrender, and Bill instantly came to his side, laying a rough hand on his shoulder.

"Nothing," Douglas shouted back defensively. "If a bomb went off here, someone in this group had to have planted it!"

"You're the one reaching for the gun, man," Trevor stated.

"Me?" Douglas scoffed. "I lead this team! Why would I be the traitor?"

Trevor shrugged. "I'm just pointing out the flaws in your theory."

"It's not like Hamish would blow himself up," Douglas yelled.

"I'm not dead," a man's voice trailed across the water.

Everyone's eyes darted up to spot a second figure hanging out the side of the plane.

"Hamish!" Douglas yelled, grinning. "I thought you were—"

"Yeah, well I'm not," Hamish growled back. "I've had a terrible flight and I'm starving, so can we please make a plan to get me off this blasted airplane?"

"The engine took a bit of a knock with the explosion, so Debbie's not starting right now!"

"Debbie?" Trevor asked.

"His airplane," Charlotte explained.

Oliver and Bill nodded to each other.

"Bill is going to watch these guys," Oliver whispered in his wife's ear. "Will you help me pull the plane back in?"

"Have you got some rope, Nick?" Charlotte yelled towards him.

Nick tossed a piece of rope tied to a stick at her, and Oliver helped her pull the plane in. Soon, they were welcoming Nick back onto dry land.

"What happened?" Oliver demanded.

"We came in for the landing," Nick began, his fingers still trembling as he gestured, "and something just didn't look right."

"What do you mean?" Charlotte asked.

"I caught a flicker of color under the jetty that seemed out of place. When I mentioned it to Hamish, he started freaking out."

"I didn't freak out," Hamish grumbled. "I just calmly pointed out that it might not be safe to use the jetty."

"I mean, who says that to a pilot like me? I was born for unsafe landings." Nick laughed.

"The point, Nick," Oliver interrupted gruffly.

"Anyway, I drifted up towards the jetty and tossed out one of Hamish's bags to see what would happen…"

"And then kaboom," Hamish concluded dryly.

"So they rigged the landing to blow up as soon as someone set foot on it," Charlotte said, still gripping her rifle.

"Did you bring what we needed?" Douglas asked, unable to hide the desperation in his voice.

"I brought them," Hamish affirmed, though his expression didn't match the joy he should have been exhibiting.

"What's wrong?" Trevor asked.

"The bag…" Hamish's eyes flicked towards Nick.

Douglas groaned and ran his hands through his hair.

"I don't get it," Trevor said.

"The evidence went 'kaboom'," Charlotte explained, using Hamish's terminology. "Nick tossed Hamish's bag onto the landing. They destroyed the evidence in the explosion."

"Which is exactly what the Romanos wanted!" Douglas said, kicking at the smoking rubbing on the ground.

"The who?" Oliver asked, perplexed.

"I'll explain later, I promise," Charlotte said, giving her husband a reassuring stare.

"I'm getting a little tired of hearing that line," he muttered. "I want to know what's going on, immediately."

Ignoring the glares from Trevor and Douglas, Charlotte bit her lip, uncertain of where to begin.

"Who's this guy?" Hamish asked, jerking a finger in Oliver's direction.

"I own this place, and unless someone tells me what's going on, you lot can board what's left of Nick's plane and get out of here!"

Charlotte intervened by pulling her husband away from the group and providing a quick rundown of who each person was, and how they were connected to the case against the Romanos.

"You're telling me we're housing a crew of lawyers, a grieving widow, and a child who witnessed his own father's murder?!"

"Pretty much," Charlotte said. "I did plan to talk to you, it's just…"

"I know. I haven't been around. This isn't your fault."

"One of them has to be working for the Romanos," Charlotte whispered to her husband. She shifted slightly so she could see the group behind him. Her eyes scanned each face, unable to decide whether Douglas, Trevor, or Hamish was the imposter. Of course, she disliked Trevor the most, but she worried that was clouding her judgment.

"No one else would have known where that landing was, and there's no way anyone else could have gotten here from New York without us knowing it," Oliver agreed. "It has to be one of them."

"But which one?" Charlotte's question floated between them.

As if by an answer to her question, the three men broke into a loud argument, fists flying wildly between them.

Bill, who rarely had time for male bravado, fired his weapon into the air as a warning shot. "The next one of you to swing a punch gets a bullet as a reward," he growled. "Let's go."

The three men glowered, but obeyed him trudging their way slowly back to camp. Charlotte and Oliver readied their rifles in case any of them attempted to escape.

"Is this city enough for you?" her husband retorted, just loud enough for her to hear.

Charlotte scowled at him.

Chapter 6
Watery Escape

"Where are Sandy and Nicolas?" Douglas demanded.

"They're taking a breather until I can be sure they're safe with the three of you around," Charlotte replied curtly.

Trevor laughed. "Do you really think one of us is working for the Romanos? We were at your lodge the entire morning. How could one of us have been able to rig the jetty to blow?"

"Well, technically, I was with Oliver for part of the morning," Charlotte said. "But there were times where I can't recall seeing *you* around."

"I was in the recreation room, working on the case!"

"Just because you're used to being the one firing the questions, doesn't mean you get to be rude!" Charlotte shifted her gaze. "And where were you, Trevor? You were *silent* this morning."

"I was with Sandy and Nicolas after breakfast. Then I had a date."

Charlotte's eyebrows raised in surprise. "With whom, exactly?"

"She asked me not to say…"

"Madison!" Charlotte yelled.

"Y-yes, Charlie?" Madison stammered, coming forward, frightened by Charlotte's bellowing.

Charlotte fixed her gaze on the young woman. "Were you on a date with Trevor this morning?"

Madison's big blue eyes flickered from Trevor, to Charlotte, and then back to Trevor. "Uh huh…"

"And was he with you the *whole* time?"

She hesitated for a moment. "Yes."

"Thank you," Charlotte said, dismissing her.

"Charlie," Madison blubbered pathetically, "I'm sorry. I know you told me—"

"That will be all. Thank you, Madison. Please return to the front desk."

"Look," Hamish interrupted, "it's possible the Romanos learned of my trip. The guy who handed over the tapes probably was the one who outed Alfred and had him taken out. How do we know he didn't alert the Romanos to my trip here?"

"How would they have gotten someone out here before you even arrived?" Charlotte shook her head. "I think the rat is one of you. For all I know, the jetty wasn't rigged."

Hamish blinked, dumbfounded. "What do you mean?"

"Maybe you're the rat and you bombed your own bag to blow."

"There's no proof to support your absurd theory, so we need to stop wasting time and start working on the case," Hamish snapped.

"I agree with Charlotte." Douglas frowned. "It had to be someone here. But there's no point wasting more time.

Hamish, we'll make do with the intel you've brought until we can get this figured out."

Charlotte clapped her hands together. "Great. I'll leave you to your work." She headed to the door and then paused, remembering she was the host of a lodge rather than a police detective. "Dinner at six."

"You're just leaving them in there?" Bill asked. "Do you want me to keep a look out?"

"Nicolas and Sandy are safely on the lake. No one can get to them now," Charlotte answered in a hushed whisper. "The best we can do is just let them work on their case while we wait for Nick to fix his engine. Then the bunch of them can get out of here."

"Have you spoken to the corporal?"

"I think I'll try to radio the Mounties as soon as I have a good signal. The weather must be bad on his side since I haven't been able to get through."

"Don't worry. I'll keep watch out here. You get some rest."

Charlotte sighed. "I don't like this one bit. My boy is out there on the lake with Nicolas. What if something happens to him?"

"Thomas is a smart kid. Nothing is going to happen to them. They're fine. You did the best thing you could in getting the Waters to safety."

"Thanks, Bill."

***

Hours passed and Benjamin, the head fishing guide, hadn't returned with his precious cargo—the boys. Charlotte had regretted her decision of getting the boys away from the lodge. She had initially reasoned that it would buy her some time while she figured out how to keep them safe. But now, she worried something had happened on the perilous lake.

She tried to keep calm, knowing Benjamin was exceptionally skilled on the water and that Thomas had a good head on his shoulders. More than likely, they'd gotten caught up in the scenery's beauty around them, spending a long lunch on an island eating fresh fish cooked over a fire.

"Any news?" Oliver asked, checking his watch.

"I think I'll take a boat out to see if I can find them," Charlotte said. "I'm getting nervous. I know the route Benjamin took though, so it should be easy enough."

"Take a guide with you. I would come along, but I think I should keep an eye on the group here—and both hands on my gun."

Charlotte stood on her tip-toes and gave her husband a goodbye kiss her on the lips.

"Be careful," he said, concern softening his dark eyes.

"I will."

***

Charlotte shielded her eyes from the setting sun as she scanned the waters ahead of them. "See anything?" she asked the guide.

"Not yet. This was Ben's planned route for today, so we'll find them, Mrs. Bouchard. Don't you worry."

Charlotte sighed and resumed her role as watchman. "I think I see something," she announced, pointing off-course and into the far distance.

The guide shook his head. "Benjamin wouldn't have gone so far off track."

Charlotte's fingers anxiously gripped the side of the boat. "I know, but let's just check it out anyway, please." A few minutes later, she released a breath she hadn't realized she'd been holding. "It's one of ours," she said, recognizing the familiar logo on the side of the boat, even though it was just a yellow smudge from their distance.

The guide sped towards it, slowing down once the boat was in clear sight.

Charlotte frantically tried to peer inside, knowing there should have been four figures waving at her. Not just one. "Something's wrong."

"Charlotte!" Sandy shouted at her. "Thank goodness you came!"

"Sandy, what's wrong? You were supposed to be back an hour ago. Where's Ben?"

"He's here!" She gestured to the bottom of the boat with a trembling hand.

As Charlotte's boat neared the side of the second boat, she could see that there were only two people inside. Her eyes darted around desperately for the two children that weren't there. Benjamin lied motionless at the bottom of the boat, and Sandy was practically tearing her hair out in panic.

"I don't understand!" Charlotte cried. "Where are the boys? Where is Tom?" She scuttled over into Benjamin's boat.

"They're gone!" Sandy wailed, grabbing at Charlotte's arms. "We were attacked!"

"*Attacked*? By who?"

"I couldn't tell," Sandy sniffed. "He was wearing a mask. I don't know how he found us, but he did. He went straight for…"

"Straight for what?"

"For Nicolas!" Sobbing, Sandy dropped her face into her hands.

Charlotte gripped her arms. "Sandy, I know your heart is aching, but I need to know what happened. My son was here too."

"Benjamin is alive!" the second fishing guide called. "He has a nasty bump on his head, but he'll make it."

"Thank goodness." Charlotte breathed a sigh of relief.

"Our boat was anchored while the boys were fishing. There was no escape," Sandy said, her voice strained. "Benjamin tried to fight him off, but the man whacked him in the head with an oar." Sandy took a deep breath, trying to gather her emotions before continuing. "The man charged at Nicolas, and Thomas went on the attack. He got a well-aimed kick in, causing the man to drop Nicolas. Then, in a flash, Thomas grabbed Nicolas by the collar and pulled him overboard!" Her eyes were wide as she relived the trauma.

"*What?*" Charlotte gasped. "Can Nicolas swim?"

"He's not a poor swimmer, but they never would have made it to shore!"

Charlotte scanned the water to judge the wind's speed and strength. "How long ago did this happen?"

"About an hour ago," Sandy guessed.

Charlotte nodded, her mind racing as she turned back to the guide. "Get Sandy and Benjamin back to the lodge, and have Oliver check them out. Thomas knows these waters and where the islands are located. There's a good chance he got them back to shore."

"It's not possible," Sandy stated hopelessly. "There's no way they could have survived!"

"You don't know my Thomas." Charlotte rushed over the edge into the second boat and charged off where she estimated the attack had taken place. The shore wasn't too far, especially since there was an island stop midway, where they could have regained their strength before the last stretch. Charlotte followed the line to the shore, but there was no sign of the boys anywhere.

She knew she would have to continue her search on foot, but with daylight fading and the absence of a weapon, she would have to make a quick stop at the boathouse to get emergency supplies.

Twenty minutes later, Charlotte set out on foot with a flashlight and a rifle. She knew Oliver needed to stay at the lodge to make sure that Benjamin and Sandy were okay, and to contact Corporal Dumont about the attack.

After thirty minutes of trudging along the shoreline, Charlotte began doubting the accuracy of her estimates. Her mind replayed Sandy's account of the story. It made little sense. If the Romano gang was so ruthless, why not take out everyone in the boat to get to Nicolas? Yet, they'd left Sandy untouched, and the man had remained masked. It just didn't add up.

Charlotte froze, swearing she'd heard something. She clicked her rifle into place and scanned the bush line around her. She was never sure how far her enemy wolves strayed, but she would hate to come across the entire pack around dinnertime.

The trees rustled in the wind, and a branch nearby snapped off and fell to the ground.

Charlotte tried convincing herself that her mind was borderline hysterical and couldn't be trusted to judge her surroundings.

Taking a deep breath, she continued her walk.

Just when she was giving up, she spotted muddy footprints leading up from the lake. Her heart skipped a beat as she dropped to her knees to study the child-sized prints. Overjoyed, she nearly wanted to kiss the ground.

Re-energized, Charlotte kept going, her eyes fixed on the two sets of footprints leading into the woods. She broke into a smile when her nose caught a whiff of cooking fish. "Tom!" she shouted, running through the trees towards the faint glow of light.

"Mom? I'm here!"

Charlotte pushed through a bush and ran straight into the arms of her damp oldest son. "My baby," she cried into his hair. "My brave, brave boy…"

"Mom, I need to tell you something…" He pulled himself away from her. But Charlotte was focused on surveying every inch of him, ensuring he was unharmed. His skin was pale, his lips were tinged blue, and his clothes were still soggy from his icy swim.

Noticing a black bruise forming on his cheek, Charlotte caressed the mark. "What happened to you?"

"Charlie," a little voice squeaked next to her, "Thomas said you would find us!"

Charlotte threw her arms around the child who wasn't her own, but hadn't deserved the lifetime supply of misery he'd endured in his brief existence. "I thought you'd be safer out on the lake," she cried as she hugged the two boys. "This is all my fault. I'm so sorry –"

"You did what you thought was right," a man's voice cut in.

Charlotte jumped and spun around as a shadowy figure emerged from the dark and into the firelight. "Trevor? What are you doing here?" Yet, immediately after asking she knew the answer.

Nicolas quivered at her side, and Thomas's sharp intake of breath confirmed that Trevor was the rat.

Trevor had planted the bomb on the jetty.

Trevor was the masked man who'd tracked down the boat so he could destroy Nicolas.

"Why?" she said, the question falling stupidly between them.

Trevor smirked as he slowly advanced, the faint metallic click of a gun revealing that he was armed and had intentions to kill.

Charlotte spotted her own rifle on the ground a few feet away. Upon finding the boys, she'd dropped her weapon to hug them. In hindsight, she couldn't believe how stupid she'd been in not picking up the telltale signs of the stalking through the woods. It may not have been an animal predator tracking her, but the signs were still the same and she'd led the wild predator right to his intended prey.

"You won't get away with this," Charlotte yelled. "Let the boys go. They've done nothing to deserve this."

"How very brave of you, Charlie. I didn't think those big, brown eyes had it in them to stare at me with such hatred. You're even more beautiful when you're angry."

Charlotte was disgusted, but knew she had to maintain her focus if she wanted to get out of alive. "So, you're the inside man for the Romanos?" she said, hoping to at least gain a confession during the encounter.

Trevor shrugged. "I wouldn't say I'm on anybody's side, but they can buy my loyalties for the right price."

"You disgust me. So, what's your plan, Trevor?" she asked, watching him circle her. "Kill us? Then what? Go back to camp and pretend nothing's wrong, like some kind of sick psychopath?"

"Oh, I will not kill you," he said with a nasty sneer. "I'm just going to make sure you're wounded enough for the wolves to do the job for me."

"How cavalier of you," she retorted dryly, although she sensed they were running out of time. "Too bad it won't work."

He scowled. "All right, Charlie-knows-better-than-anyone-else. What's the flaw in my plan?"

"Didn't you know?" Thomas scoffed, catching on to what his mother was doing and joining in. The two of them laughed.

"Know what?" Trevor demanded, shifting his weight uncomfortably, his fingers twitching on the trigger.

"Wolves don't eat humans. That's just in the movies to scare people," Charlotte said, displaying absolute confidence in her own lie.

"Fine. Then I'll shoot you first and see if the wolves aren't tempted by your appetizing flesh," Trevor grumbled, his face contorted with hatred.

Charlotte sighed. "That won't work either, I'm afraid."

"They can hear gunshots for miles," Thomas explained. "They'll know it was you!"

Trevor kicked at the dirt, annoyed that a fourteen-year-old boy had outsmarted him. "Well, maybe I'll just strangle you to death." He shoved his gun into his waistband and advanced on Thomas, thrusting his hands towards the boy's neck.

Charlotte had been waiting for this enraged lapse in judgement. With all her might, she swung her fist into Trevor's nose. Yet, a gunshot resounded at almost the precise same moment.

Charlotte jumped and checked her body for a wound but found none.

A voice sounded out of the surrounding darkness. "Touch the boy again and you're dead," Bill's husky voice growled out of the shadows, not an ounce of bluff in his threat. He stepped into the firelight, ominous shadows dancing across his face.

Trevor scowled but raised his hands in surrender, nevertheless.

Noticing his eyes flick down to the gun tucked in his belt, Charlotte promptly snatched it out of reach and tossed it into the bushes.

Trevor roared in frustration, his hands balling into fists as if he wanted to strike her.

Bill stepped forward and pressed the barrel of his gun into Trevor's back.

"Thanks, Bill," Charlotte said, full of relief. She gathered the shaking Nicolas into her arms and felt Thomas's fingers worm into her free hand.

All the while, Bill kept a tight leash on their convict the entire walk back to the lodge.

Despite her tirade of questions, Trevor refused to say another word, causing Charlotte's thoughts to drift toward Bill instead.

She couldn't help wondering about the mystery that was Bill. He had appeared out of nowhere, and yet, he always seemed to sense when any of them were in danger. She had subdued her burning curiosity for some time, but from the moment he'd stepped in and saved not only her own life, but that of her son as well, she knew she needed answers.

Chapter 7
Catching Rats

"Thank you for coming all this way, Corporal."

Oliver stepped forward to shake the young corporal's hand.

"I'm only sorry that I couldn't get here sooner," he apologized, removing his hat to smooth down his hair.

"Please, come inside," Charlotte said. "I know you're here on business, but we've got some refreshments waiting for you."

The corporal grinned. "That would be appreciated."

The group entered the lodge, chatting amongst themselves. Two boys scampered up the stairs behind them, clearly in awe of the corporal's bright red uniform.

Once inside, Corporal Noah Dumont listened to the series of events that had befallen the Northern Getaway Lodge. His blue eyes surveyed Sandy as she recounted what had happened on the boat. He listened without interruption, except to ask a question.

Noah Dumont calmly absorbed everything. He was a young corporal; some even felt him too young for the position. But the region had a lot of ground to cover, and there'd been a shortage of Mounties in the area during the eighties. Despite the heavy task that fell on his shoulders,

Corporal Dumont did what he could in the name of justice, rising to the challenge with surprising strength and dignity. It wasn't often that the Bouchards got to welcome him in person at the lodge, but when the situation was grave enough to warrant his presence, he came without fail.

"I'd like to talk to Thomas and Nicolas, please," Noah informed Charlotte.

Thomas and Nicolas, who'd been watching the proceedings from a corner in the room, scuttled to the front.

"Nice to see you again, Thomas," the corporal greeted him with a smile. "You've grown taller."

Thomas offered a nervous grin. "Thank you for coming out all this way to help us."

Noah laughed. "With your mother around here, you don't seem to need me all that much!"

The room chuckled, and Oliver threw a loving arm around his wife's waist.

"And you must be Nicolas Waters," Noah said, turning his blue gaze to the younger boy.

"I like your buttons, Corporal," Nicolas said. "They're so shiny."

The corporal chuckled and nodded. "Let me tell you a secret." He lowered his voice to a whisper. "I really like my shiny buttons too."

Nicolas and Thomas laughed, the tension flowing off of them.

"Now," the corporal's face grew serious, "I hear that you're the two brave young men who stood your ground in the face of danger."

"That's not true," Nicolas said. "I was as scared as anything. I think I would be dead if it weren't for Thomas and the others who helped."

Noah smiled. "It takes a lot of courage to admit something like that, Nicolas. Now, do you know who attacked you on the boat yesterday?"

"Trevor," Nicolas replied firmly.

"But I believe the man was masked," Noah recounted. "At least that's what your mother claims."

"He was masked, but I know his voice. I used to spend a lot of time with my dad at the office when he wasn't working serious cases, so I know Mr. Trevor's voice very well."

"Is there anything else that makes you so sure it was him?"

Thomas cleared his throat. "Sorry, Corporal. May I add something we noticed?"

"Of course, Tom. Go ahead."

"I recognized Mr. Trevor's clothes. He wears this thick gold chain all the time, and that was visible during the fight. And he also had on the same spotted socks from breakfast. Plus, he wears too much cologne. I would know that smell anywhere." Thomas's nose crinkled.

Charlotte suppressed a proud giggle in awe of her son.

The corporal raised his eyebrows. "Those are some excellent observations, Thomas. I'm really proud of you both for noticing all of those things. It's immensely helpful in identifying the criminal here."

"It's definitely him," Thomas stated. "And if you want to make absolutely sure it's him, check for a bite mark on his ankle and bruises round his... uh... upper legs. I got in a good kick and bit him as hard as I could on his ankle."

Smiling, the corporal folded his arms and surveyed Thomas. "You sure take after your mother. I think I've just found the perfect career for you."

"*Really?*"

"How would you feel about enrolling in the Royal Canadian Mounted Police?"

Thomas's eyes beamed with excitement. "That would be the best thing in the whole wide world!" He flashed a quick look at his mother and father to check if they approved.

"We just have to wait until you're a little older," the corporal added, since it looked as though Thomas was ready to pack his bag and leave already.

Thomas giggled euphorically.

"Thank you for your help," the corporal concluded, shaking each boy's hand.

"Why don't you see what Chef Victor has prepared for dessert?" Charlotte suggested. "I heard he needs some expert chocolate mousse tasters."

Nicolas and Thomas shared a look that spoke volumes before darting out the room.

"There's one more person I'm curious to talk to," the corporal announced.

Charlotte raised an eyebrow. "Oh? Who might that be?"

"Bill," Noah said. "His name cropped up a few times in your interview, and yet, I've never even met him."

"I'll see if I can find him," Charlotte said, her stomach twisting. "He helps us around the lodge. We couldn't manage without him."

Charlotte wasn't sure why she felt impelled to defend Bill, but she did. Shortly after meeting him for the first time in the woods, a strange man by the name of Rick Neilson had come in search of him. Charlotte had tried, but it was a name she couldn't forget. Sometimes it woke her from her sleep, as though the wind whispered the dreadful name through the trees. Rick had seemed like a rich, out-of-town bag of trouble. He'd claimed Bill used to work for him and was indebted to him. When Charlotte had refused to acknowledge Bill was staying at the lodge, Rick became very aggressive and threatened her.

Sadly, that wasn't the last time she'd encountered Rick. He had visited again, locating Bill and trying to force him onto his private plane. When Bill refused, Rick turned hostile and pulled a weapon. Charlotte had fired her own weapon, and Rick finally scampered off like the pestilent rodent he was, never to be seen again—or so she hoped.

A wave of anxiety flowed through Charlotte's every limb as she watched Bill, who they knew so little about, take a seat in front of the corporal. Deep down, she knew her anxiety stemmed from not wanting to lose Bill.

"Bill…" Noah began, waiting for a last name.

"Just Bill," he stated, undeterred by the bright red uniform jacket.

Charlotte chewed her bottom lip, not so sure how well the corporal would accept the half-baked answers.

"All right." Noah nodded, a slight crease forming on his brow. "Where are you from, Bill?"

Bill looked shiftily out of the window. "What does this have to do with the investigation under way?"

Charlotte hid her face behind her hand.

The corporal shifted in his seat slightly, his red uniform jacket creasing across his front. "How did you know Charlotte was in danger?"

Bill nodded slowly, as if deciding whether this was a safe enough question to answer. "I didn't like any of these bigshots city people since the day they arrived, except for young Nicolas. When I heard they were missing and saw Charlotte head off from the boathouse with a rifle in her hand, I knew something was up. While I was fetching my gun, I saw that man called Trevor sneak out of the bushes and follow her. So I knew trouble was underway."

"Why didn't you call for back up?"

"Mr. Oliver was already in the lodge, making sure everyone was safe there. At that stage, we didn't know who the rat was. I had my suspicions, but who am I to say anything? If I'd first taken the time to find someone, I might have lost the trail and been too late to help Ms. Charlotte and the boys," Bill answered defensively.

"Rightfully so," the corporal agreed. "I wish I knew who you really were so I could thank you properly. You did a great service to our country by saving Charlotte and the boys. You did what I couldn't, and I'm indebted to you for that. I'll include what you've done in my report, though I wish I could give you some kind of medal instead."

Bill chuckled. "That won't be necessary."

Noah Dumont extended a hand and Bill shook it.

Charlotte felt herself breathe for the first time since the interview began.

"Well, I think I have everything I need from all of you, so let me speak to the defendant and then I'll be out of your hair," the corporal said.

Charlotte watched Corporal Dumont lead Trevor out of the lodge in handcuffs, staring in horror at the red bite mark visible on Trevor's ankle.

Trevor caught her eye and glared at her.

"What will happen now?" she whispered to Oliver.

"The corporal will start the paperwork. He'll also contact the police in New York, and they'll take it from there."

"Well, it's a relief to know he won't be in the same country as us for much longer," Charlotte pointed out, her stare still burning into Trevor's back.

"I still can't believe he's a traitor," Douglas spat.

"I'm sorry," Charlotte offered, restraining from adding that she'd tried to warn him from the beginning that there was something strange about Trevor. Instead, she turned her attention back to Douglas, who looked distraught. "So, what are your plans?"

He sighed, his shoulders slumping forward. "Hamish and I will continue to work the case. We feel that our position is compromised. We don't know if Trevor ever got through on the radio to the Romanos. Backup could be on the way, so we'll leave here as soon as possible."

"That's understandable," Charlotte said. A part of her was relieved by the prospect of the group leaving. Yet, another part of her felt a strange sense of sadness over not seeing things through.

Nick shook his head. "You won't be going anywhere for a while, I'm afraid. My plane isn't up for a long trip. She needs some replacement parts. I'm going to try doing a short flight to Uranium City and scratch around for some spares around there."

Douglas' eyes filled with panic.

"Don't worry, Doug," Charlotte soothed. "We can keep you safe here until you have to leave. The lodge is well protected and difficult to access without the principal routes being aware of traffic coming this way. The corporal will put out an alert to stop any unauthorized planes flying in our direction."

Douglas shook his head. "You don't know the Romanos or what they're capable of. Look at Trevor. He was a good man, and they turned him, just like that."

Charlotte bit her tongue, reserving her judgment for another day. "Well, you better crack on with the case. I'll see how I can help Nick."

"Thanks, Charlie. I don't know what we would have done without your family."

Chapter 8
Ghost Town

Charlotte had tossed and turned the entire night, unable to sleep after the series of strange events that had befallen the lodge. One thing that especially plagued her, as it had many previous sleepless nights, was Bill's reluctance to answer questions.

The man had saved her and Thomas's lives, but she didn't even know his last name. Bill had crept into their family almost overnight, and each of them dearly loved him. Even Oliver had slowly softened and accepted the strange old man as one of them.

Yet, when interviewed by the corporal, Bill had put up a wall of defensive so strong, Charlotte had felt like she was staring at a stranger rather than a man she trusted around her children.

She had tried questioning Bill herself, but he refused to answer her questions and simply sauntered away as though it had stricken him deaf.

Then there was Rick Neilson, who had invaded her family's privacy and safety to track down Bill.

There was just so much that didn't add up. All Charlotte knew was that Bill had left Uranium City and found them.

By dawn, she'd decided about how to spend her day. As much as she loathed flying with Nick, she joined him on his trip to Uranium City.

***

Charlotte stared open-mouthed at the abandoned buildings, devoid of warmth, sound, and life. It had only been a couple of years since the mine had shut down and the city's inhabitants had fled to more lucrative prospects, but Charlotte could have never imagined the deep depression that had engulfed the once thriving hub of activity.

Weeds and bushes sprouted through the cracks in the tarmac. Stray cats scampered away behind rusted nuclear transport trucks and empty drums.

Charlotte passed what looked like a former school building, its walls filled with shattered windows that led to desolated classrooms. They had boarded other buildings up, but she swore faces peeped out between the cracks. "This is awful," she mumbled, scuttling closer to Nick.

"Yeah, it shocked me the first few times," he admitted. "But you know what I admire about this place?"

"What could you possibly admire? This place is a tragedy!"

"People are survivors," Nick explained. "This city saw the greatest prosperity followed by the greatest economic collapse. Most fled, leaving behind everything they'd built up. Others had no other option but to stay, and they've made do with what they have. For them, this is home. The community is rather..." he paused while searching for the correct word, "special. Each person living here has an astounding story to tell."

Charlotte looked around the abandoned streets with fresh eyes. They had walked from the outskirts into the center, and she slowly saw that life existed. A small community of survivors went about their daily business, enduring as best they could despite their changed circumstances.

"It's pretty amazing when you think about it," Nick continued. "It makes me proud to be a human, you know? Makes me think we can survive anything."

"Bill didn't survive here," Charlotte mumbled.

"Oh, but I think he did. I think he just longed for a family, so he went in search of one."

Charlotte kept her thoughts to herself, unwilling to reveal her real reason for wanting to come to Uranium City. "Why don't you see what spares you can rake up, and I'll have a look around," she suggested, her eye catching a lone figure in the distance she thought she might try talking to.

"If you want to learn more about Bill, the pub is a good place to start." Nick winked.

"What? I said nothing about —"

"I know you didn't accompany me today because you enjoy my flying. I can see that Bill has made quite an impact in your little home. And I know you, Charlie. You want to know who you're bringing into your circle."

Charlotte studied the young pilot who believed in aliens, wore his heart on his sleeve, and should have died a thousand times after all the stunts he'd pulled in the air. She couldn't help appreciating the rare moment of empathy he'd just displayed. "Thanks for understanding."

Nick grinned. "If you really want to thank me, you'll put in a kind word for me with Madison."

Charlotte rolled her eyes good-naturedly and shooed him away so she could find her way through the strange town.

"Are you lost?" an older woman asked her.

"Hello," Charlotte greeted with a friendly smile. "I haven't seen this place since the mines shut down."

"It must be quite a shock then." The woman chuckled. It creased her face with wrinkles, likely because of the stress of surviving in a city that had economically burned to the ground.

"It is… I came with the pilot, Nick."

"Oh." The woman laughed again. "Yes, I know Nick. He's quite the sweetheart to an old woman like me, always bringing kind words."

Charlotte hid her surprise and nodded. "He respects the residents who stayed behind."

"It's more than that. Nick looks beyond the hideous wreckage and into the heart."

Charlotte remained silent while she pondered this unusual observation about a man she'd regularly judged to be the complete opposite. She had always seen Nick as the guy who was attracted to a pretty exterior and not much more.

"Anyway, that's not what you came here to talk about, is it? I'm sensing you're here for information. Your eyes are afire with curiosity."

Charlotte smiled guiltily. "I have a few other questions."

"Go ahead."

"Do you know a man called Bill?"

"It depends why you're asking," the woman responded with hostility, immediately going on the defense.

"I mean him no harm," Charlotte replied quickly.

"You're not the only one to claim that. I have no information for you." She turned away from Charlotte and resumed her work.

"Please, ma'am," Charlotte pleaded. "If the other person you're referring to is Rick Neilson, I'm not on his side. I'm looking out for Bill."

The woman froze, her beady eyes refocusing on Charlotte. "How do you know Rick?"

"Rick found his way to my lodge on Lake Athabasca." Charlotte lowered her voice. "He claimed he wanted to help Bill, but I didn't trust him. Let's just say that he and I aren't friends…"

The woman relaxed.

"The only reason I'm asking about Bill is because he lives with my family now," Charlotte continued. "I have three beautiful children who love him… I love him too. He's wormed his way into our hearts, but I know nothing about him, and I just know something is *very* wrong."

"You're right," the woman said in a low voice. "Bill is trouble. I knew him here, though he won't remember me. He was always under the influence of alcohol. Bill appeared from nowhere, a mountain man that kept to himself. I'm glad he finally found himself a home."

"I thought he worked on the mine here?"

"Not to my knowledge, but you can check in at the old office. They have some archives."

Charlotte nodded slowly, shocked at just how many lies Bill had told. She had assumed the few questions he had answered had at least been truthful, but that clearly wasn't the case. "Why do you say that Bill is trouble?"

"He seems wrapped up in a shady past that only Rick Neilson knows about, and anyone who keeps company with Rick is bad news."

"Can you tell me more about Rick then?"

"He's a terrible man." The woman shook her head.

"I've worked out that much," Charlotte said. "What makes him so dangerous?"

"I blame him for what happened to Uranium City," she spat, tears welling in her eyes.

"Did he have something to do with the mine shutting down? I thought that decision had come from higher up?"

"Rick had a hand in it," the woman hissed. "He made it happen somehow. I know he did."

Charlotte sighed. "Look, I know firsthand that there'd been a lot of deaths over the years. My husband's father was one victim. The mine took too many lives, and that's not including the countless cases of people who suffered quietly from radiation."

The old woman shook her head, deep creases forming in her brow. "You don't know," she complained. "You don't know what Rick is capable of. He has so much money. He was one of the few who didn't lose a dime when the mines gave out. In fact, he got *richer*. Explain that!"

Charlotte's frustration grew. She had little time to spend talking to the woman, and she failed to see how any of her information unveiled the mystery that was Bill. "Did Bill work for Rick?"

The woman shrugged. "That, I don't know. Bill just appeared one day. Rick saw him and was furious. They had a big fight in the pub, and Rick dragged him out."

"Do you think that's why Bill left Uranium City?" Charlotte asked, clawing desperately at the hope of finding answers.

"I can't answer that. Rick seemed almost afraid of Bill. He couldn't bear to see Bill out in public. I never could understand what was between them. I think Bill left in search somewhere to belong."

Charlotte nodded. It was the same explanation Nick had given her.

"I need to make my way home," the old woman said, dismissing their conversation.

"Wait, I have more questions," Charlotte begged.

"Maybe you'll find some answers at the pub." She pointed a bony arm toward a dilapidated building.

Charlotte waved the woman off and glanced back up the road, readying herself to face more strangers. The door swung open, and rowdy music accompanied a staggering figure out into the street before the door shut again and stifled the noise.

Charlotte braced herself and stepped inside. The music seemed to cut the second she entered, and every eye drew towards her, despite being few.

Cat calls and singing broke out as the men welcomed her inside.

"What can I do for you?" the bar tender asked, drawing her away from the intrusive eyes of the intoxicated group.

"I have a few questions," Charlotte began, taking a seat at the bar.

"Usually, it's considered good manners to order a drink first," the bartender explained with a stern look.

"Sorry," Charlotte said. "I'll have a beer, please."

"There we go." He smiled. "Now, what do you want to know?"

The room grew quiet, as if every person in the bar also wanted to know.

"I'm Charlotte Bouchard," she began.

"Bouchard." The man pensively stroked his impressive beard for a moment. "Why is that name so familiar?"

"We run the lodge on the edge of the lake about twenty miles from here. I flew in with Nick."

The bartender nodded slowly. "Ahh, okay. I've heard of that lodge. A lot of tourists like to come and gawk at our misfortune. They always speak very highly about your lodge, but that's not where I've heard the name before."

"Perhaps you knew my husband's father, Malik Bouchard? He worked on the mine here many years ago."

"Malik!" The bartender snapped his fingers. "I never met him, but I've heard the story. A real tragedy when a loved one is lost. Well, Mrs. Bouchard," he continued with renewed respect, "it's an honor to have you visit us."

"Thank you," Charlotte smiled, embarrassed by the man's sudden warmth. "I just have a few questions. I'm trying to find out more about a man called Bill."

"Why?" The man's demeanor changed just as the old woman's had.

"I know him, and he's a very dear friend. I'm worried that he's in trouble."

The bartender chuckled. "Bill *is* the trouble. Be careful who you let into your life."

"Why do you say that?"

"Bill had an unquenchable thirst for the drink. He practically paid my salary with the amount he drank here daily."

"I'm aware of that," Charlotte said. "He's much better now, though. Hasn't had a drop in two months."

The bartender raised an eyebrow. "He must care for you very deeply if he could choose you over the bottle."

Charlotte looked down at her beer, distracting herself with a sip.

"There's a second reason Bill is bad news though," the bartender continued, folding his arms.

"If it's to do with Rick Neilson, I know about him too," Charlotte said, hoping to speed the process so she could get some information she didn't already know.

The bartender glared at her.

"Sorry, I didn't mean to be rude. I just have limited time. What I really want to find out is what Rick Neilson has on Bill? What makes Rick such a bad guy around here?"

The bartender tilted his head, his eyes gazing over her shoulder. "Why don't you ask him yourself?"

The bell above the bar's entrance chimed as a new guest entered.

Charlotte slid off her chair and scurried around the side of the bar, cowering under the counter.

The bemused bartender looked down at her for a second before greeting the latest customer. "Hey, Rick. I had an old friend of yours in here asking about you."

"Really?" came the familiar voice. "And who might that be?"

The entire bar fell silent once again. Charlotte could feel the floorboards reverberate as footsteps approached the bar.

"Oh, just someone from out of town," the bartender's boomed. "She was asking about old Bill."

"My good friend, Bill," Rick's crooned. His footsteps pounded until his colossal, dirty boots were right in view and the intrusiveness of his cologne burned Charlotte's nose. "Hello, Charlie," he said, smirking down at her.

"Hi, Ricky," she greeted with equal tenacity, scrambling up off the floor. "I thought I would come snoop around your part of the woods. You know, return the favor…" Her words were met with a round of laughter from their spectators.

"Charlie, if you have any idea who I am," Rick threatened, "I advise you mind your own business. For your own safety."

"I've heard some interesting stories around town about you," Charlotte bluffed. "I wonder if our Corporal Dumont has ever had the pleasure of meeting you?"

"For the sake of your three beautiful children, I *really* hope that you're lying," he growled.

"Now, now," the bar tender interrupted, "I don't want any trouble in here."

"There won't be any trouble," Charlotte assured, her eyes fixed on Rick. "I'm leaving, anyway. There's a sudden stench that just filled the air in here, and I can't stomach it much longer."

"That's just his cologne," one of the drunk residents bellowed, causing a chorus of high-pitched cackles and laughter.

Charlotte scampered away before Rick could lay a hand on her. He looked murderous, but she was tired of the fear he seemed to cast on people, and refused to bow to it.

Nick was waiting for her outside the pub. "Whatever will I tell Mr. Bouchard?" he teased. "Of all the places you could frequent, you chose *that* one?"

"You told me to go to the pub," Charlotte retorted. "I could've died in there!"

"Well, in my defense, I didn't know Rick Neilson was in town."

"You know Rick?"

"I know *about* Rick," he corrected. "Anyway, the plane is all sorted, and it looks like a storm is on the way, so we had better test her out."

Charlotte gulped. "*Test* her out?"

"It'll be fun!" Nick enthused, a mad twinkle in his eyes.

Chapter 9
Wolves

It was a bumpy flight, but the plane held it together and a thrilled Nick brought them in for a safe landing.

"Thank you for today. I actually enjoyed my time with you," Charlotte said with a smile. "You're a pretty decent guy, Nick. I'm glad I got to see you in another setting."

"Was that almost a compliment from Charlotte Bouchard?" Nick said, grinning widely. "Thanks for giving me a shot."

"I'll be putting in a kind word for you with Madison. You've earned it by my standards. Now, I'm sure the chef has cooked up a storm. Why don't you see what's left in the kitchen?"

"What about you?" Nick asked, unable to remove the grin from his face.

"I think I have someone I need to talk to."

Nick nodded and disappeared into the dusk.

Meanwhile, Charlotte made her way to Bill's cabin.

"You had quite the adventure today," Bill mumbled from his porch once Charlotte was within his view. "I figured you would stop by."

Charlotte's eyebrows shot upwards. "Why is that?"

The frown on his face was visible in the flickering lantern on the porch. "Don't play coy with me. It wasn't hard to figure out what drew you to Uranium City."

She sighed. "Bill, I just wanted to know more about you. You've become one of us, and yet, I know nothing about you."

"So you investigated me, like you did Trevor. Were you happy with what you found out? Should I expect the corporal anytime soon?"

"Not really," Charlotte said, sensing that it hurt him. "Besides, I would rather hear it from you. And you know I would never call the corporal on you."

"Stop digging."

"Why?"

"You won't like what you find."

"Just tell me the truth. I know you didn't work on the mine like you said you did."

He sighed. "I didn't work in the mine, but I worked for Rick."

"Doing what?"

Bill grimaced. "I'm not proud of the work I did for him, but he paid me a lot of money, so I did it. Anyway, as time went by, I got out. It scared Rick I would tell the truth about him. He threatened me, so out of fear, I ran away. And that's how I ended up on your doorstep."

"But why not go to the corporal and tell him the truth? That way, you could have been free of that atrocious man."

"I can't do that..."

"Why not?"

"Because I gave him my word. I'm part of the wrong Rick committed. Outing him means outing me, and I'm not ready to accept the consequences just yet."

Charlotte bit her tongue. She had never thought of Bill as a coward before, and despite the words coming out of his mouth, she still didn't think of him as one. Hence, she knew there had to be more to his story than he was telling.

"Why do you care anyway?" Bill asked.

"Because you're one of us now and we care for our own."

He shook his head, and when he spoke, there was a bite in his voice. "I think you can't help yourself. Snoop around in things until you find answers."

"Bill, I don't want Rick around here again. If he comes in search of you and endangers my children, I'll have to do something about it."

Bill was suddenly alert, his eyes fixed on hers as he jolted forward in his chair.

"What?" she asked, confused.

"Why did you mention the children so specifically?"

Charlotte blabbered for a moment, struggling to find the right words.

"You saw Rick, didn't you?" Bill accused. He leapt to his feet and started pacing angrily.

"I did," Charlotte confessed. "It wasn't my plan, but he found me."

"I bet he did, with all the questions you were asking. Do you have any idea the danger you put yourself in?!"

"Am I in danger now?" she countered, her voice testy.

"What?" Bill halted. "Of course not. I would never hurt you." His voice softened. "But looking into Rick is like playing with fire. Stay away from him."

"Okay, I will," she promised.

"And if he so much as threatens the hair on any of the kids' heads, I'll see to him myself," Bill grumbled through gritted teeth. He then sank back into his porch chair and fixed his gaze on the stars.

Bill's angry outburst assured Charlotte that he was truly on their side and would never intentionally hurt them, which gained him enough trust in her eyes to satiate her curiosity for a while.

They sat in silence under the stars, the peace between them suddenly broken by a high-pitched scream.

Bill and Charlotte scrambled to their feet, instantly alert. Bill grabbed his rifle from inside the cabin and Charlotte took the lantern.

The scream echoed from one of the guest cabins.

"Help me!" a youthful voice yelled.

"That sounds like Nicolas," Charlotte said. She bolted towards the guest cabins on top of the hill, leaving the older Bill behind.

As Charlotte neared the cabin Sandy and Nicolas had been sleeping in, she froze, her blood chilling in her veins.

A blood-thirsty snarl ripped through the night air, sending shivers down Charlotte's spine. She rattled the lantern around and discovered a wolf low to the ground, his fur in hackles as deep growls ravaged through his system.

"Woah!" she said. "I will not hurt you, buddy..."

The wolf advanced on her.

"Charlie," Nicolas's voice squealed from inside the cabin, "they're in here too!"

Her stomach twisted at the thought of Nicolas surviving rogue city gang members, only to be torn to shreds by a murderous pack of wolves.

"It's okay, Nicolas," she called to him. "Stay calm. They can smell fear."

When she heard Nicolas gulp, she realized she had probably given him the worst instruction possible.

Bill finally caught up. He stopped, held his breath for a moment as he steadied his rifle, and aimed at the wolf.

"Bill, don't!" Charlotte yelled, cowering away from the wolf as the gunshot echoed through the camp site.

She opened her eyes and saw that the wolf had scampered away to safety, his fur still raised around his neck as he growled at them.

"I would not kill him," Bill said.

The wolves inside the cabin had darted out at the sound of the gunshot, pursued by a howling Nicolas. He bolted straight for Charlotte's leg and gripped her tightly.

She lifted him up, and he clung to her like a monkey, his tiny frame quivering. "I thought they were going to eat me!" he wailed into her shoulder.

"It's okay, honey. You're safe now. They just wanted to see what you were. Wolves are curious creatures, that's all."

"But how did they get in?"

Charlotte looked gravely at Bill, who got her meaning instantly and climbed the cabin steps to investigate.

"Was the door locked?" she asked.

"Yes!" Nicolas insisted.

"You're sure you didn't fall asleep with it unlocked and maybe the wind blew it open?"

"No! Mommy would never do that to me!"

"What do you mean?" Charlotte asked. It suddenly dawned on her that Nicolas had been alone in the cabin. His mother was nowhere to be found.

"Mommy put me to sleep with her singing. But I woke up when I saw her leaving the cabin. She said she was going to get me some milk to help me sleep."

Charlotte hugged him tightly while he continued to sob on her shoulder.

Bill caught Charlotte's eye. "Come and have a look at this."

Charlotte gently stroked Nicolas's back to calm him while she carefully climbed the stairs.

Bill gestured to some marks on the top of the porch.

"What's that?" Charlotte asked.

Not wanting to frighten Nicolas, Bill mouthed the word 'blood' to Charlotte.

Her eyes widened as she looked at the bloody wolf-prints on marked the floor. "Do you think someone injured one of them?" she whispered.

Bill shrugged. "Maybe. But if one was injured, why were they here hunting?"

"You don't think your shot could have ricocheted and struck one of them, do you?"

"No. You can see where my round hit the dirt at a safe distance away."

"This is strange." Charlotte frowned.

"What's strange, Charlie?" Nicolas asked in a hoarse voice. His crying had slowed, but his body was still shaking.

"Nothing, Nicolas. Don't you worry your sleepy head. Maybe we should go inside and get your mommy, okay?"

"I'd rather stay with you, Thomas, and Mr. Bill, if that's okay?"

Charlotte shot Bill another loaded look as she cradled the cowering Nicolas.

"What's going on?" Oliver shouted, running towards them. "I heard a gunshot!"

Behind him, a bewildered group of people had emerged from the main lodge. Douglas was standing next to Madison. Sandy pushed past Hamish the moment she saw Charlotte holding Nicolas.

"Mom," Thomas's voice drew her attention. "What's going on?"

"Tom, take Nicolas to the kitchen and ask chef to make you both some hot chocolate," Charlotte ordered.

Thomas, knowing his mother's various tones and the degrees of urgency in which they were used, promptly obeyed, grabbing the reluctant Nicolas by the hand and leading him inside.

"Everyone else in the recreation room, please."

"I just have one question," Charlotte said to the group of perplexed faces. "Why was Nicolas sleeping alone in his cabin?"

Sandy dropped her gaze to her shoes.

"It's my fault," Douglas spoke up. "I was supposed to be watching him tonight. But I had... other plans."

"What kind of other plans?" Sandy snapped. "You know how dangerous it is for my Nick at the moment!"

The awkward silence was broken with a piercing snort, followed by a tirade of sobs that Charlotte had heard in her office on many occasions. "Madi," she said, dreading her friend's next words.

"We were on a date," she cried.

"You know the last time you said that you were on a date with someone, he was actually out stealing a boat and trying to kill Thomas and Nicolas."

"I know," she howled. "But this time, Douglas and I really were on a date!"

"It wasn't really a date," Douglas interjected. "I just needed someone to talk to. I've been under a lot of pressure, and Madison is a good listener. That's all it was."

"I thought you said it was a date?" she snapped at Douglas. "I wore perfume and everything! Do you know how hard it is to get perfume all the way out here?"

"I don't have those kinds of feelings for you," Douglas said, pulling at his collar. "We've only just met, for crying out loud!"

Madison turned her back to him and folded her arms.

"All right," Charlotte said. "That explains why you weren't in the cabin with Nicolas. But what I don't get is where were you?" she directed her question at Sandy.

Sandy's eyes bulged. "I was inside working on the case with Hamish. They figured out that the Romano's son was close to someone on the opposition, which meant there was a traitor. And the tape recordings my husband was trying to secure revealed who that was. Hamish thought I might help him figure out who it could be."

"I thought the traitor was Trevor?" Charlotte said.

"We thought so too," Douglas interrupted. "But I worked with Trevor for years. His betrayal was very recent and likely because of money rather than any kind of friendship with the Romano gang."

"The Romanos aren't the only danger out here," Charlotte said. "Nicolas woke up to a pack of wolves breathing down his neck. They had left the door unlocked and somehow, the wolves got it open. He could have been killed in his sleep."

The room descended into an icy silence and shortly thereafter, Sandy started crying and Douglas looked like he'd seen a ghost.

"I swear, I locked it!" Douglas said.

"Don't look at me," Sandy hissed. "I put him to bed and locked him in. You were the last one out there, or so I thought." She glared at Madison.

Charlotte sighed. "Look, nothing happened, so why don't we all get a good night's rest and tackle things in the morning? But I just have to warn you all, please be more vigilant. Once you're in your cabins for the night, no walking around. Understand?"

Everyone nodded grimly.

"Nicolas will sleep with us in our cabin tonight," Charlotte informed Sandy. "He won't leave Thomas's side after this. Besides, we sleep with rifles in our room, so that might reassure him that no wild animal, or other predator, will get to him."

It wasn't really a question, and Charlotte didn't give Sandy a chance to protest. She proceeded to the gun safe, where she unlocked her rifle and escorted her son and Nicholas back to their cabin.

Chapter 10
More Rats

Charlotte was up before the rest of her cabin after another relatively sleepless night. She kept imagining waking up to a wolf gnawing on her toes.

Nicolas and Thomas had crept into her room in the night, dragging a mattress to the foot of their bed. Slowly, the mattress had been transformed into an entire blanket fort. Before she knew it, there was a chorus of giggling children inside a heap of squirming blankets. Discovering the fun, her other two children joined Thomas and Nicolas.

They had no idea Charlotte was just as grateful to have them there with her, as they were grateful to be there.

She dragged herself into her office, eyed the heap of paperwork on her desk, and hurried away to grab more coffee before attempting to face the day.

When she reentered her office for the second time that morning after a lengthy discussion about breakfast with Chef Victor, Charlotte noticed a faint buzz from the radio that hadn't been there thirty minutes before. Frowning, she moved closer to examine it. They had changed the frequency to one she didn't recognize, and it was warm from being on.

Someone had used her radio to make a call.

Charlotte sat down in her chair, cradling her coffee mug and staring wide-eyed at the radio, her stomach turning in knots as she wondered who had been using her radio.

A light tap on her door drew her away from her dark thoughts. "Charlie?" came the familiar voice.

"Yes, Madi," she answered stiffly.

"I was hoping to catch you alone so we could talk…"

"I'm not sure we have much to talk about that we haven't discussed a hundred times before," Charlotte said, biting her tongue so she said nothing more in anger.

"Look, I know I messed up, and I'm not here to give you a long list of excuses about how I'm just trying to find the right guy."

"Oh?" Charlotte retorted, genuinely surprised.

"There's something that's really bugging me," she continued, nervously twisting her hands as she spoke. "It's about Douglas."

Charlotte sighed. "Of course, it's about Douglas."

"We weren't together the whole time last night," she admitted, her face crimson. "He disappeared for a bit and about thirty minutes later, the gunshot went off."

"You think he went and unlocked the cabin, leaving Nicolas as prey for the wolves?" Charlotte asked.

"He said he just had to use the restroom, but I don't think that's true because I used the restroom while he was gone and there was no one else around." She burst into tears.

"This isn't your fault," Charlotte said, her mind racing.

"It is! I attract killers and criminals to this lodge!"

"That's not true," Charlotte scolded. "Look, Madi, I need you to focus for a few seconds. Do you recognize this radio frequency?"

"That's New York," Madison said, confirming Charlotte's worst fears.

"Someone radioed out," Charlotte stated in horror.

"And you think it was Douglas?"

"I don't know." Charlotte bit her thumb anxiously. "There's one way to find out."

***

The group was seated around the breakfast table, chatting and laughing while they poured coffee and fought over the crispy bacon Victor had just brought in.

"So, who radioed New York?" Charlotte asked, interrupting their moment of peace.

"W-what?" Douglas stammered. "What are you talking about?"

"One of you snuck into my office this morning and used the radio. They set the frequency to someone in New York."

Douglas, Hamish, and Sandy all stared at each other in open-mouthed shock.

"Charlotte, we don't know what you're talking about," Douglas said.

Charlotte leveled a heated stare at him. "What about when you left Madison last night to go to the restroom?"

Douglas narrowed his eyes on her. "What are you implying?"

"You left just in time to lure a pack of hungry wolves into Nicolas's room. You're the second rat in this group!"

Douglas's chair crashed to the wooden floor as he threw it backwards. "How dare you! I love that little boy as if he were my own!"

"You're the one behaving suspiciously, Doug! There has to be another traitor in this group. Why else are there still attempts on Nicolas's life?"

"Look, last night was an accident," Hamish interjected. "Can we all just calm down? Douglas is no spy. He's in this as much as Alfred Waters was. I'll stake my life on that."

"Where is Nicolas?" Sandy asked, as if it had finally occurred to her she hadn't seen her son that morning.

"Probably eating breakfast with Thomas," Charlotte notified her rather crisply.

As if by clockwork, Rebekah entered the room with her usual pale expression whenever a child escaped from her lessons. "Charlie," she whispered, "I need to talk to you."

Charlotte shook her head, dreading the words she already knew were coming.

"Thomas and Nicolas disappeared from my lessons this morning."

"Rebekah, seriously! Can't you keep them under lockdown for *one* day?!"

"I'm sorry!" Rebekah cried. Used to a calm and collected Charlotte rather than an exhausted, anxious wreck who'd already lost her temper three times in the same morning, Rebekah ran from the room.

"Did she say my child was missing?" Sandy said, stepping closer.

"It happens," Charlotte retorted. "It's not the end of the world."

"Oh, really?" Sandy folded her arms and jerked her head at her. "Because here you are, with all the tenacity in the world, daring to accuse us of trying to murder Nicolas. Yet you've gone and lost him!"

"Thomas often goes exploring," Charlotte said, trying to restore her calm. "He likely took Nicolas with him. I'll start tracking them."

"Oh no," Sandy waved a finger in Charlotte's face. "I no longer trust you with my child. You fill his head with strange ideas. I'm coming with you."

"I'm coming too," Douglas announced, stepping forward.

"No, Doug, I think it's best if you and Hamish stay here and keep working the case," Sandy said.

***

Twenty minutes later, Charlotte was hiking through the familiar woods around the lodge. She stopped at regular intervals to search for spoor or other prints that might alert her to her son's whereabouts. Usually when Thomas did this, he would leave tiny signs for his mother to track.

"Looks like you do this often," a red-faced, out-of-breath Sandy commented.

"Thomas loves the outdoors. Usually, when he has to deal with something difficult, this is where he escapes to."

"Don't you worry something will happen to him out here?"

"I do," Charlotte admitted. "Thomas is smart though, and he reads nature well. Plus, he has an air rifle. It doesn't kill, but the noise is enough to scare away predators."

"I would never allow Nicolas out of my sight if I lived here," Sandy snapped.

"But you live in the city. I used to long for the busy life where I could grab a hotdog and coffee on the corner and catch a cab to work. But I'm thinking I'm perfectly happy here."

Sandy walked a few steps in silence while she weighed Charlotte's response. "It's more peaceful here," she admitted. "But I would rather my child grow up exposed to the problems of authentic life, rather than being sheltered in some make-believe world out in the middle of nowhere, where you don't even have telephone lines."

Charlotte bit her lip to stop herself from responding rudely. "Maybe you have a point. We're rather sheltered out here, but I think we protect my son from a lot of repulsive traits that the real world seems to throw about daily. What's more important than growing up to be a good person?"

"Yeah, well, life in the city isn't easy like it is here. If you want to survive, you have to be who you don't want to be. My husband was a good person and look where that got him."

"Sandy," Charlotte stopped walking and faced the other woman, "I'm so sorry for everything you've been through. I know I haven't exactly been easy on you while you've been here –"

"I don't need your pity," Sandy interrupted. "I'm used to surviving, okay?"

"Sorry," Charlotte mumbled, refocusing on the ground in front of her. "I found something," she announced, glad to change the subject.

"What is it?"

"A broken twig. Thomas left us a trail after all."

"Great," Sandy huffed. "Let's get this over with."

They hiked for another forty-five minutes, Charlotte tracking her son carefully each step of the way.

"Isn't it beautiful out here?" she asked Sandy, attempting to make a connection again.

Sandy shrugged, her eyes focused on the ground.

Charlotte held her hand up, and they both stopped. Though they couldn't see them yet, Charlotte could hear them giggling. "Tom, hun, it's mom," she called.

"Mom! I knew you'd find us. I need to tell you something important. We know who the —" He stopped dead in his tracks the moment his eyes rested on Sandy.

Charlotte read her son's nervous body language. "What's wrong?"

"We know who the rat is," Nicolas concluded the sentence proudly, stepping out next to Thomas. But soon, his reaction mimicked Thomas's.

"What's gotten into the two of you?" Charlotte asked, confused. Suddenly, she felt her weapon being tugged off her shoulder. "What are you —" she began, turning around. Stunned, she stared down the barrel of her own gun.

"Not so fast," Sandy ordered. "I've had enough of you, Charlotte Bouchard." She spat the name as though it was foul in her mouth. "You've been bossing us around, interrogating and investigating us from day one!"

"And rightfully so, it seems," Charlotte said.

"Shut-up! I've had enough of you! One more word, and I swear, I'll put an end to you."

"We've already been through this with Mr. Trevor." Thomas yawned. "You can't shoot us. They will hear your gunshot for miles and they'll know it was you."

"Unless I say Charlotte fired at a wolf and missed, which is why it tore out her throat."

"No one will believe that either," Thomas said.

"Why not?"

"My mom never misses."

Charlotte grinned. She had to admire her son, even if he was about to get them murdered. "So, you were also behind this," Charlotte said, trying to divert Sandy's attention so that the boys had a chance at escaping. "Is that why Trevor knew you were out on the water with the kids? You told him."

Sandy smirked. "Exactly. And it would have worked perfectly if it weren't for your stupid son."

Charlotte fought the urge to rise to her son's defense. She knew the remark was made to lure her into an irrational attack. "Were you in it for the money too, or was that just Trevor?"

Sandy laughed. "I was Trevor's money. I gave him the job. He was so easy to turn, it was pathetic."

"So that makes you part of the Romano gang." Charlotte gulped the truth in chunks, her stomach turning at the news. "Is that who you contacted using my radio?"

Sandy's smug smile provided her answer.

"We figured it out this morning," Thomas explained, casting a murderous stare at Sandy. "Nicolas saw blood on his mother's shoes at breakfast this morning."

"What?" Sandy looked down in shock, noticing the tiny red splotches for the first time.

"He remembered hearing you say there was blood outside his cabin door last night," Thomas directed at Charlotte. "Then he recalled why he was with his dad the night he was killed."

"Stop talking!" Sandy screamed. "Another word, and I'll kill Charlie, you got it?"

"Daddy took me away," Nicolas continued bravely. "He figured out that you were the one leaking case information to that gang!"

Charlotte turned on Sandy, rage filling her every cell. "You were the one? You betrayed your own husband?"

"He betrayed me first!" Sandy snapped. "Do you know how many nights I curled up alone in bed? My husband was obsessed with the Romano gang. It was all he ever talked about. He stayed out at the firm, working late night after night. And what was left for me? An exhausted man who didn't even care if I was there or not when he came home."

"I'm sorry your marriage suffered because of the case, but that's no excuse!"

"Don't you dare judge me. I was so alone… And then one day, I met Barry while out shopping. He was so nice to me. So sweet and attentive…" Her eyes grew wistful at the memories. "Barry was good to me. But it wasn't until I was in love that I found out he was Leo Romano's son. But by that point, it didn't matter anymore. He told me all the cruel things my husband was accusing his father of and how it wasn't true. I had to help."

"You were conned," Charlotte stated bluntly. "And you sold your family for him. Barry killed your husband, didn't he?"

Sandy sneered. "My husband deserved it."

"Mommy, no!" Nicolas wailed. "Daddy was good!"

"You don't understand what Mommy went through!" she yelled at her son. "You weren't supposed to be there, Nicolas. If you had just stayed with Mommy instead of running away with your father when he found out what I was doing, you wouldn't have to die!"

"Thomas, now!" Charlotte shouted, knowing he would understand what to do.

Thomas grabbed Nicolas by the arm and bolted into the trees, darting behind a rock.

Predictably, Sandy charged after them, giving Charlotte the opportunity to wrestle the rifle away from her.

Charlotte lunged with all her strength at the emotionally charged woman, throwing Sandy off her feet. As the two tussled in the dirt, kicking up dust around them and scrabbling for control of the rifle, a misdirected finger hooked around the trigger.

The crack of a gunshot ripped through the air, startling the birds resting in the tall pines and sending fuzzy squirrels scuttling for safety.

The gunshot was followed by an equally loud scream, from a young boy.

Chapter 11
A Special Visitor

Charlotte let out a sob as she broke through the last line of trees, her beloved lodge coming into view. She had never longed to see a sight so comforting as that of her safe home nestled between the breathing, swaying trees, and sparkling waters of Lake Athabasca.

"Are you okay?" Thomas asked his mother, concerned.

"I'm all good," she assured, though she'd hurt her ankle in the fight. "Come along, Nicolas."

"Can I stay here with you, Charlie?" Nicolas asked. "I never want to go back to the city."

Charlotte chuckled. "I think we must talk to Douglas about that."

"You're still my son," Sandy retorted hotly, her hands tied behind her back with some rope Thomas always carried.

"I would be quiet if I were you," Charlotte said, prodding the woman forward with her rifle.

Charlotte looked up to find her husband and Bill running up towards them. As if knowing Sandy was the real criminal, Bill grabbed her and moved her to a holding room.

"Are you okay, love?" Oliver asked, stooping to kiss his wife. "I was so worried."

"We're fine," she answered. "How did you know that Sandy was the bad guy?"

Oliver laughed. "We have a visitor you need to meet. You will not believe who it is."

Charlotte limped to the lodge and entered the recreation room to find a strange older man seated on one sofa. Opposite him sat a scowling Hamish and Douglas.

"What's going on?" Charlotte asked, perplexed.

"That's what we'd like to know," Douglas spat.

The older man climbed to his feet. Two intimidating bodyguards stepped forward from behind him. "Leo Romano." The man held out a bony hand to Charlotte.

"Excuse me?" she said.

"Leo has come to make peace, apparently," Douglas announced, though he clearly didn't believe it.

"I'm confused, Mr. Romano," Charlotte said. "You're the one who had Alfred Waters killed. I just heard it from Sandy myself. She confessed everything."

"No, my dear," the old man corrected. His voice was gentle, not at all what she imagined a vicious gang leader to sound like. "My son, Barry, is to blame for this bloodbath, though I'm not entirely innocent. I've let Barry do his own thing, without correction, for too long now. He took our family name a little too seriously. I'll admit, I had various schemes I dabbled in, but never bloodshed, and never murder."

"What does this mean for the case?" Douglas demanded.

"I won't shield Barry any longer. Alfred Waters was a gentleman, and he deserves more than what he received. Barry will pay for his crimes. I'll testify against him in court if

I have to, but he won't hide behind me like a coward anymore."

"Mr. Romano, do you really mean this?"

"I do," Leo affirmed, tears brimming in his eyes. "My son has brought shame on my family name, and with my dying breath, I'll work to clear away his mess."

"What about the drug laundering?" Hamish asked, jumping up with hungry eyes.

"That, you must talk to my lawyers about," the old man replied with a cunning smile, resulting in a round of confused, but warm laughter.

***

Charlotte and her husband sat on their porch, their feet up on the banister, whiskey in hand, and their eyes gazing up at the starry vista above them. And in that moment, Charlotte realized she was perfectly happy.

"Charlie," a little voice appeared at her shoulder.

"Yes, Nicolas, love?"

"Can you come tuck me in again?" he asked. "Thomas is already asleep, and I thought I heard wolves."

"I'll be there in a minute," she promised, getting up from her chair. She gave her husband a kiss before following their newly adopted son into their cabin.

The End

Now that you have finished this cozy mystery, please consider writing a review on Amazon. It would be appreciated.